Francis Tumblety

A few passages in the life of Dr. Francis Tumblety,

The Indian herb doctor

Francis Tumblety

A few passages in the life of Dr. Francis Tumblety,
The Indian herb doctor

ISBN/EAN: 9783337810931

Printed in Europe, USA, Canada, Australia, Japan

Cover: Foto ©Raphael Reischuk / pixelio.de

More available books at **www.hansebooks.com**

A FEW PASSAGES IN THE LIFE OF

DR. FRANCIS TUMBLETY,

THE INDIAN HERB DOCTOR,

INCLUDING HIS EXPERIENCE

IN THE OLD CAPITOL PRISON,

TO WHICH HE WAS CONSIGNED,
WITH A WANTON DISREGARD TO JUSTICE AND LIBERTY,

BY ORDER OF EDWIN STANTON, SECRETARY OF WAR.

ALSO JOURNALISTIC AND DOCUMENTARY

VINDICATION OF HIS NAME AND FAME,

AND PROFESSIONAL TESTIMONIALS

RESPECTFULLY INSCRIBED TO THE AMERICAN PUBLIC.

CINCINNATI:
PUBLISHED BY THE AUTHOR.
1866.

PREFACE.

———◦◦:◦◦:◦◦———

As, outside of my professional pursuits, my name, for a brief period, was dragged before the public in a manner any thing but agreeable to my mental or bodily comfort, I have, equally in unison with the wishes of my friends, and with the *amour propre* that every person of an independent spirit, and a conscientious sense of rectitude should possess, concluded to publish the ensuing pages, not only in self-vindication, but to exhibit in its true light a persecution and despotism, in my case, that would hardly be tolerated under the most absolute monarchy, and which should serve as a warning to all who believe in the twin truths of Liberty and Justice ; that eternal vigilance is the price of both, and how easy it is for unscrupulous partisans and ambitious men, when not restrained by the strict wishes of constitutional rights, with which the wise precaution of the fathers of the Republic guarded the liberties of the citizen, to trample upon the law, muzzle public sentiment, and run riot in a carnival of cruel and malignant tyranny.

My experience is, I am certain, but an isolated case among hundreds ; it may, however, serve to

"point a moral and adorn a tale;"

at least it will tend to awaken apprehension, and therefore a watchful spirit in every patriot and worshiper of constitutional liberty.

FRANCIS TUMBLETY.

(3)

KIDNAPPING OF DR. TUMBLETY.

In the following sketch, which I have deemed it my duty after mature consideration to lay before the public, I have endeavored, as concisely as possible, to present a little episode in the dark pages of our late history, in which I unhappily figured, a victim to a tyrannical disregard of the rights and liberty of a citizen, and an example of individual outrage and persecution, which would at one time have been deemed impossible of perpetration in free and enlightened America.

In the course of my narrative, it will be necessary to take a retrospective glance at my professional career, and herein I can produce such evidence of a life of ministering devotion in the cause of science and humanity, as should, even in the gangrened perversion of the most bigoted mind, have acquitted me of the slightest suspicion of those crimes of which I was, with such reckless disregard to truth and justice, accused, and for which I have been the recipient of such unlawful punishment.

Not only was my liberty ruthlessly assailed, my life jeopardized, and my property plundered, but a character, previously unblemished, was assailed with all the venom that infuriate malice could supply, by that portion of the press, who have, during the late unhappy epoch, been but too ready to applaud and justify the persecution of defenseless individuals, no matter upon how baseless a foundation the charges against them may have been preferred.

There is an old Spanish proverb to the effect that he who has injured will never forgive you, and so far as my experience has been, of late, it is perfectly correct; for even after the cruel blunder, in my case, was known, and I was set at liberty, I sought in vain an exoneration through the same channels in which I had been so maligned and abused. They repudiated the old manly system of fair play; they had wantonly assailed me, and even when convinced that not the slightest taint attached to my character or fair fame, they remained silent. They had propagated and pre-judged a slander which was proved to be false as the father of evil, but they persevered in their dastardly meanness by refusing the *amende,* and only to that portion of the press who had never assailed me, am I indebted for sympathizing with and placing me in my true position before the public.

In the course of my narrative, it will be necessary for me to refer to scenes and events beyond the period of my unjustifiable arrest, and this I deem essential in order to produce such evidence of my antecedents as must satisfy the most prejudiced of my previous blameless character and pursuits, as well as to elucidate a clue to the persecution and wrong of which had been the victim.

I had been practicing my profession in Canada with distinguished success, and, in the course of a prosperous career, I accumulated an equal amount of profit and of fame. So far as the latter went, I trust the reader will not deem me an egotist, when I state that in the British Provinces I had acquired the respect and consideration of the first citizens, in proof of which I was importuned by an influential body to represent them in the Colonial Parliament, in opposition to the celebrated Thomas Darcy McGee, a gentleman whose literary and political reputation is well known in this country.

In order to substantiate this position—for I do not wish the public to take my word upon credit—I will here introduce some documentary evidence, which must speak for itself.

In the year 1857, after being waited upon by a delegation representing a large body of Canadian citizens, urging me to enter the political arena, a course which my habits and my inclination strongly repudiated, and which I declined, it was rumored that I was nevertheless about to become a parliamentary candidate, and paragraphs to that effect found their way in the Canadian press. One of many I have before me. It was in the *Union*, Ottawa City, and reads as follows:

" It is hinted that Dr. Tumblety will offer himself as a candidate on grittish principles, in case of a vacancy in this constituency, and that he is now feeling the pulse of the people. The Doctor having amassed a fortune in the treatment of all ' the ills that flesh is heir to,' in which treatment he has ever been successful, now philanthropically proposes to devote his brilliant abilities to the cure of the dangerous · diseases affecting the body politic, and is proudly conscious of the success that awaits him in the effort."

The report was circulated so universally, that I deemed it incumbent to put forth a public disclaimer, which appeared in the Montreal *Commercial Advertiser*, of Dec. 7, 1857, of which the following is an extract:

Sir: I notice in your valuable journal of the 3d instant, a short paragraph, in which it is intimated that it is my intention to offer myself, at the ensuing election, as a candidate to represent the suffrages of the people of Montreal, in opposition to D'Arcy McGee, and that I am about to receive a most numerously-signed address, and, I may add, have resolved to come forward for the representation of the Irish interest. In allusion to the above statements, I may say that it is not my intention at this present time to contest an election, but I have every hope, were I to do so, of ultimate success.

I have merely recalled the above, in evidence that my position at that time, in the city of Montreal, was such as to induce what I conscientiously believe to have been a majority of the voters to offer me their suffrages in a " parliamentary contest."

But without the circle of politics, I am enabled to invite attention to certificates in that country from the highest and most influential people—ladies and gentle; men of the first standing in society, whose names are a guarantee of genuine and unsolicited evidence. In this connection, it will only be necessary to enumerate a comparative few in the long catalogue, who voluntarily came forward as indorsers of my high professional standing, and the efficacy and success of my treatment:

SIR E. HEAD, *Governor of Canada.*
HON. HY. STERNES, *Mayor of Montreal.*
HON. GEORGE HALL, *Mayor of Quebec.*
HON. JOHN HUTCHINSON, *Mayor of Toronto, C. W.*
HON. J. B. ROBINSON.
HON. JAMES CUMMINGS, *Mayor of Hamilton, C. W.*

Hon. W. Matthews, *Mayor of Brantford, C. W.*
Hon. W. Baker, *Mayor of London, C. W.*
W. Savage, *Colonel of Artillery.*
H. P. Dwight, *Sup. Montreal Telegraph.*
J. Taylor, *Justice of Peace, Toronto, C. W.*
R. H. Cook, *Alderman, Toronto, C. W.*
J. Urquhart, *Surgeon, Toronto, C. W.*

To these, it will not be out of place to add the sub-joined, from Hamilton Hunter, Esq., the editor of the London *Atlas*, a man of much literary culture, and whose reputation as a high-toned, honorable gentleman is recognized throughout the Canadas:

Dr. F. Tumblety—*Dear Sir:* As you are about to leave this city for some time, permit me to offer my testimony as to the very great measure of success which has attended your labors here, as a medical practitioner, during the few months you have resided among us. It has come under my knowledge that many persons laboring under diseases of longer or shorter standing, have been relieved by you, while your urbanity and gentlemanly character have won for you the good opinion of those who have made your acquaintance, and fully sustained the high reputation which you brought with you from Rochester, as embodied in the splendid testimonial which you carry with you from such a large number of the most influential and intelligent of your fellow-citizens. Wishing you every success, I have the honor to subscribe myself yours, very truly,

Hamilton Hunter,
Editor of the London Atlas.

I will not weary the reader with additional testimony of my Canadian antecedents, professional and social; that which I have adduced, will, I presume, satisfy the most skeptical of my position and respectability.

Selfishness is unfortunately the governing principle of human nature, and it has been truly said that the generality of mankind are more desirous for their own personal aggrandizement than for the happiness of those around them; hence the secret of the opposition of those who, adhering to the old-beaten track, simply because they have not the intellect or the spirit of research to explore the new and voluminous regions unfolded by nature, turn persecutors and hurl invective and anathema against their more adventurous and successful brothers.

My Canadian reminiscences are of the most pleasant character; personally I was respected, while my professional career was marked with such success as to render my name famous from one end of the Province to the other. The efficacy of my treatment was subscribed to by even the greater portion of the medical faculty, whose prejudice against what they deem an innovation upon the old-established routine, is remarkable throughout the world.

My friends of the press were lavish in their encomiums, and frequently indulged their poetic fancy in complimentary effusions, among which, the following, from the St. Johns (N. B.) *Albion*, is a humorous sample:

DR. TUMBLETY.

Dr. Tumblety rode a white steed
Into St. Johns in its time of need,
Determined to cure with herbal pills
All the ailing of all their ills.
Dr. Tumblety had a greyhound—
A beautiful animal I'll be bound—
The dog looked up in the Doctor's face
As he rode along at a slapping pace.

Tumblety had a killing air,
   Though curing was his professional trade,
Rosy of cheek, and glossy of hair,
   Dangerous man to widow or maid.
Eschewing beef, and mutton and pork,
   Like Daniel of old, he fatted on pulse;
His thumb the knife, his finger the fork,
   He lived on herbs, and moss and dulse.

Of simples all he knew the use;
   He also knew the use of the weed;
But, ah! he played the dickens and deuce
   With doctors who physic, and purge and bleed.

Cures he had wrought of each disease
With healing herbs and barks of trees;
Simples culled from mountain and glen,
Plucked from the moor or dragged from the fen;
The mandrake, elm, and bitter bog bean—
Sarsaparilla and horehound, I ween—
Butternut, colt's foot, and Irish moss,
The bark of the widow and garlic sauce—
With these the Doctor's wondrous skill
Each killing disease was sure to kill.
Gouts, consumption, and shivering ague,
Deathly diseases—complaints that plague you;
All things nasty, for which physic's given,
Out of you soon by these herbs will be driven;
See certificates, given galore—
Citizens all, at least three-score:
Blind and lame, who walk and see,
Given up by the doctors, twenty-three,
All grown sound and healthy by taking
Medical potions of Tumblety's making.

So all the cramped, rheumatic, and stuffed,
Seeing how the Doctor was puffed,
Besieged his door at morn and noon,
Blessing their stars to have met such a boon

> Of a doctor who knew their disease without telling,
> Whether by seeing or only by smelling;
> Thousands came, who went assured,
> Satisfied all, for all were cured.

I left Canada a short time prior to the breaking out of the war, and visited New York, where I speedily became known in my professional capacity, as the following communication from the Board of Commissioners of Health, transmitted, with the document mentioned, from the Mayor's Office, will show:

BOARD OF COMMISSIONERS OF HEALTH,
MAYOR'S OFFICE, NEW YORK, *March* 18, 1861.

FRANCIS TUMBLETY, M. D., FIFTH AVENUE HOTEL:

Dear Sir: Herewith do I transmit a copy of Health Laws and Ordinances, published under the auspices of our commission. Inasmuch as you are a member of the medical fraternity, I have no doubt that it will prove valuable to you. I have the honor to remain respectfully, your most obedient servant,

LOUIS E. HOPKINS.

I have testimonials at this period, without number, of my successful treatment, and my name therewith frequently appeared in the public journals. About this time, an old friend, of Buffalo—A. McDonnell, an eminent lawyer—wrote me, and from his letter I make the following extract:

My Dear Friend: I perceive by the papers that you continue to astonish the natives. God and your own indomitable will have furnished you with a marvelous healing art, perhaps unequaled by any other man of your age now walking this earth. You can never want so long as you have your reason with such advantages.

One of my first introductions in Washington was to General E. C. Carrington, from the Hon. Judge Wm. F. Purcell, as follows:

Allow me to introduce to you Doctor Tumblety, of this city, a gentleman of great science, etc.

And, again, it was but a short time before I became in extensive practice, and my services were required by the most distinguished people of Washington. Among my patients were the following:

J. Gideon, one of the most wealthy men in Washington; Colonel Grandin; Mrs. Captain Balch, wife of the distinguished officer of the United States Navy; E. B. Kenley, one of the members of General Casey's staff; Mrs. Traphagen, one of the *elite* of the society of Washington, and associated in the proprietary of the celebrated Arlington property, the late residence of General Robert E. Lee; Edward Fry, Engineer of the Brooklyn Navy-yard, and Mr. Boman, one of the most prominent bankers of the city.

From Judge Joseph Bryan of Alabama, who was sojourning in Washington, I received the following:

Dear Doctor: I want to see you very much, for I want you to prescribe for me, as I feel that I must die unless you can help me. I do hope to see you to-day. Yours, very truly,

JOSEPH BRYAN.

The result of this was a series of successful visits to the Judge, and an after-continuation of respect and friendship.

I think that I may safely affirm that no person was better personally known in and around Washington than myself; and thus the absurdity of confounding me with the notorious individual for whom I was arrested, will be strongly apparent. Nay, not only in Washington, but in every city throughout the United States, as well as the British Provinces, I am recog-

nized; for there are few places in which I can not be
identified by some of my former patients, who, I am
proud to say, I am always gratified to meet, for the
feeling has ever been reciprocal.   I am not like the
physician who figured in the following humorous fable,
conceived by some imaginative genius, who evidently
was not favorably impressed with the healing ability
of the profession.   It runs thus, as near as I remember :

An individual whose wife fell sick, was gifted with
a supernatural vision, or second-sight; that is, he could
see the spirits of the departed as they re-visited this
sublunary sphere.

Anxious for his wife's recovery, he hastened to the
most renowned doctor in the city, but at the threshold was appalled by the crowd of disembodied spirits
flitting around, and he retired in dismay, for he discovered that they were the departed patients of the
physician.   He next visited the houses of the other
practitioners, but was deterred from entering by the
appearance of like spectral visitants, although less in
number.   At length he chanced upon a modest-looking
domicile, at the door of which there was but one
spirit, and thus re-assured, he summoned the doctor to
the aid of his wife.

She died, however, when the unfortunate medical
man began to bewail his bad luck; "for," said he, "I
never had but one patient before, and he, too, I was
so unfortunate as to lose."

But to return to my narrative.   And here, I will, in
the style of Hamlet, request the reader to "look upon
that picture, and then on this," and then ask himself
how it was possible for Stanton's myrmidons to mis-

take me for the notorious Dr. Blackburn, whose person is the antipodes of the following description, which was embodied in a military pass I obtained, during the memorable period of martial law, in 1865.

"Age, thirty-two; height, six feet; eyes, blue; complexion, fair; hair, dark; occupation, physician."

I will venture to assert that the only point of resemblance between myself and the individual on whose account I was so fearfully victimized, is in the last item; otherwise, I am rejoiced to state, we have no nearer likeness than "I to Hercules."

Time passed, and in my quiet but arduous professional career I had no cause for regret, when commenced that gigantic struggle which for four years drained the life-blood of the republic, while Europe looked on aghast, amazed at the sudden transition of a vast, flourishing, and peaceful country to a huge camp and battle-ground, where armies were raised and disciplined with a celerity that perfectly confounded the European tactician, and battles were fought upon a scale, compared to which many of historical magnitude in the old world were mere skirmishes.

When General McClellan was appointed commander of the Army of the Potomac, I partially made up my mind to tender my professional services as surgeon in one of the regiments, and I had the assurance from head-quarters that they would be cheerfully received; and here it may not be out of place to state that, although I have strictly avoided mixing in the political maelstrom which has proved so disastrous to the universal country, my feeling and sympathy have ever been with the Union and the Constitution, under which

Young America progressed in strength, power, and wealth, with almost miraculous growth.

Entertaining these sentiments, it will be seen how ill-deserved was the treatment I have since received from the representatives of a Government for the perpetuity of which I contemplated the sacrifice of a lucrative professional practice, and, if necessary, my life.

At this period, I was furnished by Gen. McClellan with passes to go and come where and when I pleased. I mixed with the officers of his staff, was always cordially received, trusted, and I can conscientiously lay my hand upon my heart and affirm before my Creator, that I never betrayed any trust or proved false to any friendship that I have professed.

Through a distinguished officer with whom I became acquainted in Boston, Massachusetts, I was introduced to the late lamented President, with whose gentle and genial manners I was charmed, and for whom, until the day of his ruthless assassination, I entertained feelings of the warmest respect and admiration, even as I now, and ever shall, reverence his memory.

Under these circumstances, it was inflicting insult as well as injury upon me to suspect for one moment that I could be privy to any conspiracy against the Government, or that I was familiarly associated with the miscreants who plotted the assassination of that great and good man; and yet I have been accused and suffered, but I have placed the account of my persecution where it belongs, and Heaven, in its good time, will enable me to turn the tables upon my enemies.

The prominent position I held with the Washington

public was not without its annoyances, as the follow. ing report, clipped from a Washington paper, will show:

On Saturday afternoon, a charge of libel was preferred before Jus. tice Johnson, by Dr. Francis Tumblety, against Mr. George Perceval, the proprietor of Canterbury Music Hall. Dr. T. charges that George Perceval did, on the 7th instant, and on divers other occasions, utter and publish a false and malicious libel, to the great injury and detriment of his reputation as an authorized physician.

The complainant (Dr. T.) exhibited to the Justice a programme of the amusements of Canterbury Hall, in which one of the farces pro- posed to be performed was entitled "Dr. Tumblety's First Patient." The publication of the same in this connection, the Doctor very positively stated, was intended to ridicule him and his profession, and to bring into disrepute his character as a physician. He said that he had previously requested the proprietor of the Canterbury Hall not to use his name on the stage in a burlesque performance. The Doctor also exhibited his diploma, to prove that he was a regu- larly-authorized physician, and a gold-medal testimonial to his effi- ciency as a physician, which he had received in Canada.

The Doctor, who, by the way, is a very handsome man, is rather eccentric and odd in his manner, appearing at times on the streets dressed as an English sportsman, with tremendous spurs fastened to his boots, and accompanied by a pair of greyhounds, lashed together. His skill as a physician, however, is undoubted, his practice in Washington being very extensive, and among the higher classes of society.

The upshot of this little affair was, that Mr. Perce- val was held to answer, my object not being to perse- cute, but to uphold, in my own person, the dignity of the medical profession.

A reminiscence of a more pleasing character lays before me, in the shape of a testimonial from one of the most eminent and skillful physicians in America, Dr. Thomas N. Gray, of the Carver Hospital, Wash- ington. It reads thus:

2

I have much pleasure in bearing testimony to the successful manner in which Dr. Tumblety has treated some cases with which I am acquainted, and I may add that I have always found him to be a gentleman, honorable and upright in all his transactions.

TٍHOS. N. GRAY, M. D.

WASHINGTON, D. C., *Dec.* 15, 1862.

The commendation of such men as Dr. Gray is priceless, for it can not be purchased with gold. My sojourn in the city of Washington, which embraced a period of over two years, is replete with many delightful reminiscences, and with the exception of the little unpleasant episode brought about by the manager of the Canterbury Hall, not a solitary event occurred to ruffle my pleasant stream of life.

This Perceval, by the way, has since figured extensively under the name of Leonard Grover, as an *impressario* of the German Opera. It is to be hoped that when he abandoned the low phase of entertainment dispensed at the Canterbury, and embarked in high-art pursuits, his perception of the amenities of life underwent a corresponding change.

General Wordsworth, who was well acquainted with my family in Rochester, invited me repeatedly to his head-quarters to dine with him. He was then the Provost-marshal, or Military Governor of Washington, and his quarters were at the house of General Robert Lee, on Arlington Hights. There were many pleasant reunions, at which I became acquainted with several United States officers of high rank, who have since recognized the old social time with their continued friendship. I very often remained there until it was quite late, and at such times the General invariably sent some of his staff officers with me, for my protection, to Willard's Hotel.

With one of these, Captain Bacus, who I think is a near relative of the General, I had the honor of an intimate acquaintance and personal friendship. He had been previously well acquainted with my brother, in Rochester.

As to my professional reputation, there are few practitioners who can produce such gratifying evidence of successful treatment as myself. I have the certificates of Judge Purcell of Washington, one of the oldest and most accomplished members of the Bench, whose son was treated by me with the most salutary effect. Also, of G. B. Clark, Esq., a prominent gentleman of the Post-office Department. Mr. Rogers, clerk in the Senate, who is reputed to have been a great pet and favorite of Daniel Webster and Henry Clay, and whose talent and gentlemanly bearing constituted him an ever-welcome visitor at the houses of the *elite* of Washington, was so successfully treated by me, that he gave me letters, commending my professional ability, to several Congressmen of his acquaintance. I have, too, a flattering testimonial from the Rev. Father Egan, a distinguished Catholic priest in Washington. From the Hon. Judge Smith, of Frederick City, Md., I was furnished with the following:

I have been under the treatment of Dr. Tumblety for some time. When I first applied to him, he described precisely my complaint and feelings without asking any questions whatever, and I am mending in health under his treatment, and recommend him to the public.

But I have no space for further enumeration. It will suffice that my treatment extended to the families of the very first people of Washington; that in two years I realized upward of $30,000, clear of all expenses.

I was a constant attendant at the President's levees, and often at such times I have made valuable and cherished acquaintances—among others, that of Gen. Blenker, whose many invitations to dine with him, I have still in my possession, cherished mementos of the past.

I remember an anecdote told me upon one of these occasions by the General, which will be found characteristic of Secretary Stanton, who really, as far as my experience goes, does not possess a friend in the intelligent or unselfish of any political party. General Blenker had an interview one day with the President, at which Stanton was present, and in the course of conversation, he, the General, had occasion to speak of McClellan in somewhat favorable terms, when Stanton, whose countenance darkened with the expression of a fiend, turned upon him and remarked, with a bitter sneer, that if he heard any more such commendations of a man he hated, he would procure his (Blenker's) discharge.

About this period I experienced a decline of health of an alarming character, which induced me to abandon my project of entering the army, and seriously contemplate a trip to Europe. In the mean time my relation with the President was of the most gratifying character, and as I informed him of my projected trip, he kindly furnished me with letters, one of which was an introduction to Mr. Adams, the American minister at the Court of St. James. Circumstances, however, caused me to abandon the idea, and some time after my professional duties called me to St. Louis, where I speedily established a reputation, which I regret, for the credit of the majority of the medical practitioners of that city, excited in them a feeling of jealousy that subsequently lent itself to the persecution of an innocent and unoffending man.

I have been charged with eccentricity in dress, but I presumed, as this is a free country, that so long as a person does not outrage decency or propriety, he has a perfect right to suit his own taste in the color and fashion of his garments. It seems, however, that I was mistaken, and even my partiality for a fine horse and a handsome dog—weaknesses which must be constitutional in my case, as I am happy to know they are in many of the most amiable individuals in this and every other country—has, in connection with the cut of my apparel, furnished sufficient foundation, in the estimation of the might-is-right party, to annoy and persecute me.

I was informed of some eligible landed property for sale, near Carondelet, in Missouri, and one day I visited it with the intention, if it suited me, of making a purchase. While there, I was unceremoniously arrested and incarcerated for two days, for no other offense, that I could learn, than that I was "putting on foreign airs," riding fine horses, dressing in a semi-military style, with a handsome robe, high patent leather boots, and spurs; that I kept a large greyhound, sported a black mustache; and, in short, as one of my gallant captors affirmed, "You're thinking yourself another God Almighty, and we won't stand it."

However, as there was neither treason, murder, arson, or any other hanging or penitentiary crime in all this, and as I fortunately had an influential friend at hand, I was, after, as I have said, an imprisonment of a couple of days, set free, once again to resume my professional labors, much to the chagrin of my medical rivals, to whom, as I was informed by the chief of police, I, in a great measure, was indebted for my arrest.

But I was destined soon to fall a victim to another and more serious annoyance, or, to call it by its proper name, tyrannical and monstrous persecution.

The news of the assassination of President Lincoln was flashed along the telegraph wires, and spread an universal gloom over the length and breadth of the land. I, who had known and esteemed him for his many amiable and social qualities, felt, I am sure, the great national loss as keenly as any; and from an innate respect to the man, and in sacred reverence to his memory, I attended his obsequies at Springfield, Illinois, although I could illy afford the time; for at no former period of my life was I so professionally pressed, my practice at that time netting me some $300 per day.

Almost the first person I met on my arrival at Springfield was the steward of the late President's household, who knew me at once, for he had frequently seen me at the White House, and bursting into tears, he caught my hand, exclaiming, "O, Doctor, this is a sad time for us to meet!"

The last sad, solemn ceremony performed, I returned, Heaven knows in how melancholy a mood, to St. Louis, and the day after I was once again arrested, thrown into prison, and this time my office and apartments were searched, ransacked, and plundered of every article of portable value, including a considerable amount of money. I remained incarcerated in St. Louis two days, during which period I was visited by several military officers, who, to my anxious demand for the cause of my arrest, laughingly replied, " Oh, they have such an immense amount of excitement in Washington, that Colonel Baker—under whose order the arrest was made—thinks that we ought to have a little sensation here.",

The then Colonel is now a General, but if his tyrannical proceeding toward me, and the reckless disregard he evinced to the right and liberty of a citizen, are samples of his integrity and capacity, he is as prominent a specimen of misplaced promotion as any in the service.

At the time, my arrest was thus noticed in the columns of the *Missouri Republican*, St. Louis:

Arrest of the Indian Herb Doctor.

A sensation was produced in police circles yesterday, by the arrest of the famous Indian Herb Doctor, J. H. Blackburn, *alias* Tumblety. He was arrested at his office on Third Street, opposite the Post-office, by an United States policeman, and is charged, as it is stated, with some knowledge of complicity in the late assassination of President Lincoln.

We are not informed of the grounds of the suspicion under which he has fallen. He is said to have been a former partner of Herold's, in Brooklyn, New York. A few facts in relation to the Doctor's history may be interesting in this connection.

Several years ago, at the time the practice was fashionable of giving flour and bread to the poor, Dr. Tumblety visited Buffalo, New York, and announcing to the public, through the columns of the Buffalo *Express*, that he would on the day following meet any merchant of that city on the steps of the Merchants' Exchange, and there distribute fifty sacks of flour to the poor, the proprietors of the *Express*, desiring to know more about the Doctor, telegraphed to Toronto, Canada, from which city the Doctor hailed, inquiring who he was. The answer came from the Bank of Toronto: " His check is good for $60,000 in this bank."

At the appointed hour the Doctor was present with the fifty bags of flour, which he distributed to the poor. The next day he published advertisements, and issued hand-bills, announcing that he would cure " all the ills that flesh is heir to."

Several months ago the Doctor came to this city, announcing himself as the Indian Herb Doctor, and that he was prepared to cure every known disease, and published certificates from those under his treatment.

＊　　＊　　＊　　＊　　＊　　＊　　＊　　＊

When he first came to the city, he affected a half-military dress, but upon being arrested by the provost guard for wearing military clothing, the Doctor concluded to change his style of dress.

The last portion of the above paragraph applied to the arrest I first mentioned, and for which, I was assured by the chief of police, I was principally indebted to my professional rivals, whose practice was not improved by such notices as the following, which some time previous appeared in the same paper:

We can but urge invalids and all suffering from any form of disease, to hasten and consult the Indian Herb Doctor, No. 52 Third Street, whose name has now become familiar as household words, and who will always be remembered as one of the greatest philanthropists and benefactors of the present age. The Doctor has, by his indomitable perseverance in combating and effectually curing thousands of cases of obstinate chronic complaints, established for himself a reputation which no competition can efface, nor opposition tarnish.

And again, in the *Democrat* of the same city, and about the same date, there appeared the following:

Successful Practice.—Of the numerous patients who have consulted the Indian Herb Doctor since his arrival here, several cases have come under our notice, in which his treatment is proving emi-neatly successful. Our readers have read the testimonials of Mr. McBride, the pilot; also the testimonial of Captain McClure; also W. P. Emery, Esq., of the Lindell House; also W. P. Turner, of Center Township, who has been suffering with cancer, and many others too numerous to mention. We recommend all who are suffering to call immediately and consult the Doctor.

But I am digressing from what I intended should be a plain narration of facts. The above complimentary notices are but as a drop in the bucket, to the many I have in my possession, and I only produce them here as evidence corroborative of the remark of the chief of police, that the faculty of St. Louis were jealous of my increasing fame and practice.

After a confinement of two days, during which I succeeded in discovering that beside being charged as the identical Dr. Blackburn, of yellow-fever-plot notoriety, I was also accused of complicity in the assassination of the President, I was carried to Washington, where I was thrust into the Old Capitol Prison; and without the formality of an examination, or any effort on the part of Stanton or his underlings to establish my identity with the notorious person for whom I was arrested, I was detained there three weeks, after which I was turned loose in the same reckless manner that distinguished my arrest, no examination whatever having been made of the case; nor was I afforded the opportunity, the right of every free-born man, to meet face to face my accuser, if there were such.

It was a persecution worthy the dark epoch of the middle ages, or the bloody era of the French Revolution; but time that corrects all things, will, I feel sure, enable me to obtain justice and redress.

During my incarceration, I made some new acquaint-

3

ances, among others, Governors Vance and Brown, of
South Carolina and Georgia; the Hon. Mr. Lamar, to
whose quarters I was assigned, and by whom I was
treated with respect and consideration.

While there, I was witness to much that was strange
to me, and would have been deemed incredible some
years previous. One anecdote will suffice. Myself
and fellow-inmates of this delectable institution were
prohibited looking from our bars upon the outer world.
One day we were startled by the crash of martial
music, the measured tread of a host, and the cheers
of a multitude. It was the grand *entree* of Sherman's
army. A lady, who was imprisoned for some political
offense, or at least she was charged with such—for I
had melancholy proof in my own case that being a
resident of a bastile did not necessarily imply guilt—
indulging the natural curiosity of her sex, looked from
the casement, when one of the lynx-eyed guards wit-
nessing the breach of Old Capitol Prison discipline,
raised his piece and fired, the bullet taking effect upon
a brick, a few inches from the fair one's head.

The courage and blood of the Southern heroine was
fired, as well as the rifle of the unmanly fellow; for,
shaking her fist at him, and stamping her delicate
little foot, she exclaimed defiantly, "Fire again, I
won't stir!"

At the expiration of three weeks, I was, as I have
stated, turned loose, for I can not dignify my libera-
tion with the name of being discharged, and the event
was thus noticed by the Washington *Intelligencer:*

An article from the New York *World* having been copied into the
Intelligencer, stating that Dr. Tumblety was the Dr. Blackburn who
undertook to create a pestilence in Washington, we feel it our duty

to state that the former has been discharged from arrest, and it is not believed that there is a shadow of suspicion upon him in connection with the above object, or with the assassination of President Lincoln.

The following communication and explanatory statement, written by me afterward, appeared in the Washington *Star*, New York *Herald*, and other papers:

KIRKWOOD HOUSE, WASHINGTON, D. C., *June 9.*

To the Editor of the Star:

After three weeks' imprisonment in the Old Capitol Prison in this city, I have been unconditionally and honorably released from confinement by the directions of the Secretary of War, there being no evidence whatever to connect me with the yellow-fever or assassination plot, with which some of the Northern journals have charged me of having some knowledge. My arrest appears to have grown out of a statement made in a low, licentious sheet, published in New York, to the effect that Dr. Blackburn, who has figured so unenviously in the hellish yellow-fever plot, was no other person than myself. In reply to that statement, I would most respectfully say to an ever-generous public, that I do not know this fiend in human form named Dr. Blackburn; nor have I ever seen him in my life. For the truth of this assertion I can bring hundreds of distinguished persons throughout the United States to vouch for my veracity, and, if necessary, can produce certificates from innumerable numbers of gentlemen in high official positions.

While in imprisonment, I noticed in some of the New York and other Northern papers, a paragraph setting forth that the villain Herold, who now stands charged with being one of the conspirators in the atrocious assassination plot, was at one time in my employment. This, too, is false in every particular, and I am at a loss to see how it originated, or to trace it to its origin. For the past five years I have had but one man in my employment, and he is with me yet, his character being beyond reproach. I never saw Herold, to my knowledge, and I have no desire to see him.

Another paper has gone so far as to inform the public that I was an intimate acquaintance of Booth, but this too is news to me, as I never spoke to him in my life, or any of his family.

I do hope the persons which so industriously circulated these re-
ports, connecting me with these damnable deeds, to the very great
injury of my name and reputation, will do me the justice to publish
my release, and the facts of my having been entirely exonerated by
the authorities here, who, after a diligent investigation, could obtain
no evidence that would in the least tarnish my fair reputation.

With these few remarks in justice to myself, I will close by sub-
mitting them to the public. Respectfully,

DR. F. TUMBLETY.

Dickens must have had much experience in prison
life, which he describes with the fidelity of one who
has tested the bitter ordeal of involuntary incarceration. But the experience of the great novelist has
been limited to the old barbarous system of imprisonment for debt; he never realized the horror of being
a State prisoner, and, worse than all, the State prisoner
of such a man as Stanton, under whose iron despotism
the unfortunate victim could not even speculate upon
the fate in store for him.

For three or four years, persons innocent, like myself, had been summarily arrested and made away
with, Heaven knows where, and the remembrance of
many cases I had from time to time read of, now that
I was another added to the number, crowded thick
and fast upon me. Under such circumstances, to look
philosophically upon the situation is an impossibility.
The chronicles of the past were conjured up, nor could
I glean one ray of consolation, in comparing the
tyranny of a past age with the despotism of the present. The legends of the Tower of London, the horrors
of St. Marc, the dark record of the Bastile, even the
chronicles of the Spanish Inquisition, crowded upon my
excited fancy, compared to which the Marshalsea, the

King's Bench, the Fleet, and the various receptacles for the unfortunate debtor, described by " Boz," were agreeable retreats. I remembered how men had disappeared in the bloom of manhood, to reappear years after, decrepit, furrowed, and their heads and beards prematurely whitened by the ordeal of their cruel dungeon life. In the dismal present I could derive no hope, for it seemed as if the history of the dark past was repeating itself. To the inexperienced all this may appear the effect of a morbid and overstrained imagination; but place the strongest-minded person in the situation, with an Edwin Stanton the controller of his destiny, and the incertitude of the future would unstring his nerves, were they originally of iron strength.

I left Washington, and spent some time in New York. My appearance there was thus noted by the editor of the *Sunday Mercury:*

We were honored with a visit from the celebrated Indian Doctor last evening, who has escaped the toils of the War Department, and is once more going about curing diseases with the most magical success, and threatening to send all the undertakers, sextons, and gravediggers to the alms-house. He carried in his hand a bunch of fragrant herbs, which, if introduced into the catecombs of Egypt, would set all the old mummies on their legs, as lively as before they were wrapped in their cerements. Of course he came off with flying colors, his loyalty being as genuine as his medicine. Stanton being such a malicious misanthropist, could not bear to see a benefactor at large, who robbed disease of its terrors, and is fast bringing about a millennial state of affairs when sickness will be unknown, and health and longevity be the common lot. He is again decocting his herbs, and producing lotions that make cripples throw their crutches away, and features, twisted into puckers by aches and pains, spread out into broad grins of delight. His " Pimple Banisher." will take the crimson tubercles from the nose of the most inveterate toper, and bleach

it to the hue of Father Matthew or John B. Gough. He has no
doubt of being able to cure the President, if that functionary will
place himself on the proper regimé, and substitute the juice of the
Indian herbs for that which he is in the habit of imbibing. He be-
lieves Stanton was instigated to arrest him by the proprietors of the
Greenwood Cemetery, who found that, after he located himself in
Brooklyn, the sight of a hearse in that city was as rare as the ap-
proach of a comet, and if he is not put out of the way, they will
have to convert their grounds into gardens or city lots.

The Doctor is the greatest professor of the healing art since Genius,
described by Hudibras, who could

> Cure warts and corns by application
> Of medicines to the imagination;
> Fright ague into dogs, and cure
> With rhymes the toothache and catarrh.

The intelligence of my arrest had been widely dis-
seminated; but, thank Heaven, my reputation had been
pretty well established throughout the length and
breadth of the land, and the news of my release
brought with it scores of kind letters, which I received from all parts of the country, as well from my
former patients as my more intimate friends. Their
congratulations upon my escape were mingled with
honest indignation at my groundless arrest, and the
tyranny of the individual who was at its head and
front. I still preserve this correspondence as pleasant
mementos of enduring friendship and regard.

I left the East for St. Louis, and a day or two after
my arrival in the latter city, the following appeared
in the St. Louis *Dispatch,* which was reproduced in the
Democrat:

We mentioned on Saturday the arrival of the celebrated Dr.
Tumblety, better known as the "Indian Herb Doctor," in our city,

and had the pleasure of a call from him this morning. The Doctor informs us that he was taken from his place of business in this city, last spring, and escorted to Washington. There he was told that the Secretary of War desired to see him. As that gentleman was not in the city, Dr. Tumblety was confined in the Old Capitol Prison for three weeks, and then turned out in the street, without any trial or investigation. He brings with him recommendations from the Mayor of Rochester, New York, and others, in regard to his standing in that city. As the Doctor is about to start business again in St. Louis, we mention this as an act of justice to a persecuted man.

All this was but cold comfort, and poor consolation to one who had been arrested for no crime, hurried away from a lucrative business, over one thousand miles, upon a miserable accusation that he had contemplated and been accessory to crimes of the deepest and blackest magnitude; had suffered incarceration for weeks; had been robbed and plundered by unprincipled and mercenary officials, and then finally turned loose with the cool intimation that it was all a mistake. 1 have been made the victim of a practical piece of despotism that would have been deemed an over-stretch of tyranny in the most autocratic government in the world, and for which I should have received compensation, at least so far as my immediate pecuniary losses were concerned. But no; from the time that I have regained my liberty, there has been no recognition from the proper quarter of the shame and injury that was heaped upon me, and I have even been compelled to pay at the rate of twenty cents a line, in a Government organ that had previously abused me, for the privilege of justifying myself after my release.

Among my personal friends of the medical profession, my experience has been most genial and agreeable, and upon my release from the miserable bastile ın which I had been confined, I received many letters of condolence and sympathy, of which the following may be taken as a sample:

PHILADELPHIA, *July* 2, 1865.

DR. FRANCIS TUMBLETY—*Dear Sir:* This moment I perused your epistle addressed to the *Sunday Mercury* of this city. Being a friend, I was delighted to know your whereabouts; but I have been extremely sorry to learn that you have been imprisoned by that imbecile Stanton. Yet it is pleasure to know that you have escaped the machinations of those debased sheets, which have from time to time defamed your enviable reputation. I hope our returning liberty will give you the power to bring on them their just condemnation.

It is now two years since I have seen you, but I still remember the refined and honorable gentleman, Dr. Francis Tumblety, with whom I have enjoyed many a pleasant hour; and as a proof that your enemies have not, and can not tarnish the bright luster that clings to your fair name, I write this letter, to say that your friends are unchanged.

I trust your health has not been impaired by your recent confinement, and that you are able to continue your professional duties in an extensive practice. If you visit this city, I would be most happy to see you.

I will leave here in September for Chicago, to resume my medical tuition at the Rush College.

I will be happy to hear from you at your pleasure.

With respects I am your friend,

JAS. WALTER MURPHY.

In my career, I have made the acquaintance of a really distinguished circle of people, who have acquired not only a national, but a world-wide reputation. A noble-hearted man, who, while possessing more amiability and genius than the commonality of his fellow-creatures, was also afflicted with too much of the weakness that is unfortunately often found in the gifted, the intelligent, and the generous, is conjured up in my mind's eye. In the course of my professional life, I became acquainted with Capt. George W. Cutter, a man upon whose brow the wreath of poet laureate of America should have been justly placed. He was not only a poet, but he was a hero, and upon the field of Buena Vista received the pistols and the dying message to his honored parents of the son of the illustrious statesman, Henry Clay. Both were transmitted by Captain Cutter; the first were placed into the hands of the bereaved father by their faithful custodian, and the last words of the departed hero were sorrowfully repeated. From that time Henry Clay was the steadfast friend of the man who had consoled, in his last moments, his favorite son, and I feel that the death of the great statesman was a sad drawback to the career of poor Cutter, of whom it might be said that he had no enemy but himself.

It was the old tale, a tale too often recorded, of the child of genius. Cutter's was a genial spirit, and his vices and misfortunes the offspring of congeniality. He fell a victim to drink, and in the embrace of the demon of intoxication, he fell from the lofty pinnacle that was within his reach to the depth of inebriate degradation. Many of the brightest and the best of all nations have so fallen, intellectual monuments of ruin and decay.

My prescription for a bronchial affection, which interfered with his success as a lecturer—for Captain Cutter, in the days of his popularity, was frequently invited to deliver addresses and orations—also introduced me to the celebrated John B. Gough, who was suffering under a similar affection of the throat, and who gave me flattering testimony of the healing and efficacious character of my medicines.

Poor Cutter! He was not destined to realize the harvest of his great literary genius, but posterity will do justice to the best and most original of American poets. The reader will, I am sure, pardon me for introducing here one of those brilliant gems, which, emanating from his pen, is destined to live so long as poetry exists:

SONG OF LIGHTNING.

Away! away! through the sightless air,
  Stretch forth your iron thread!
For I would not dim my sandals fair
  With the dust ye tamely tread:
Aye, rear it up on its million piers—
  Let it circle the world around—
And the journey ye make in a hundred years
  I 'll clear at a single bound!

Though I can not toil like the groaning slave
  Ye have fettered with iron skill,
To ferry you over the boundless wave,
  Or grind in the noisy mill,
Let him sing his giant strength and speed!
  Why, a single shaft of mine
Would give that monster a flight indeed,
  To the depth of the ocean's brine.

No! no! I 'm the spirit of light and love,
  To my unseen hand 't is given
To pencil the ambient clouds above,
  And polish the stars of heaven!
I scatter the golden rays of fire
  On the horizon far below,
And deck the sky, where storms expire,
  With my red and dazzling glow.

The deepest recesses of earth are mine,
  I traverse its silent core;
Around me the starry diamonds shine,
  And the sparkling fields of ore;

And oft I leap from my throne on high
  To the depths of the ocean caves,
Where the fadeless forests of coral lie
  Far under the world of waves.

My being is like a lovely thought!
  That dwells in a sinless breast;
A tone of music that ne'er was caught;
  A word that was ne'er expressed!
I dwell in the bright and burnished halls
  Where the fountains of sunlight play;
Where the curtain of gold and opal falls
  O'er the scenes of the dying day.

With a glance I cleave the sky in twain;
  I light it with a glare,
When fall the boding drops of rain
  Through the darkly-curtained air!
The rock-built towers, the turrets gray,
  The piles of a thousand years,
Have not the strength of potter's clay
  Beneath my glittering spears.

From the Alps' or the Andes' highest crag,
  From the peaks of eternal snow,
The blazing folds of my fiery flag
  Illume the world below.
The earthquake heralds my coming power,
  The avalanche bounds away,
And howling storms at midnight's hour
  Proclaim my kingly sway.

Ye tremble when my legions come—
  When my quivering sword leaps out
O'er the hills that echo my thunder-drum,
  And rend with my joyous shout.
Ye quail on the land, or upon the seas,
  Ye stand in your fear aghast,
To see me burn the stalwart trees,
  Or shiver the stately mast.

The hieroglyphs on the Persian wall—
   The letters of high command—
Where the prophet read the tyrant's fall,
   Were traced by my burning hand.
And oft in fire have I wrote since then
   What angry heaven decreed;
But the sealed eyes of sinful men
   Were all too blind to read.

At length the hour of light is here,
   And kings no more shall bind;
Nor bigots crush with craven fear
   The forward march of mind.
The words of truth and freedom's rays
   Are from my pinions hurl'd;
And soon the light of better days
   Shall rise upon the world.

But away! away! through the sightless air
   Stretch forth your iron thread!
For I would not dim my sandals fair
   With the dust ye tamely tread!
Aye! rear it upon its thousand piers—
   Let it circle the world around—
And the journey ye make in a hundred years
   I'll clear at a single bound.

But throughout my career, I have nearly always encountered the hostility of the resident physicians and medical practitioners, who, in my case at least, have not evinced any of the liberal spirit that is said to distinguish the enlightened and liberal professions.

The old faculty have ever entertained a deep-rooted prejudice against a purely botanical system; indeed, this prejudice is extended to every thing that does not suit their taste or fancy.

I am, in a great measure, the disciple of Abernethy, especially in his horror of cutting, unless as a last recourse. That great physician was the cotemporary of Sir Astley Cooper, but there was no sympathy in their mode of practice, and he at all times expressed abhorrence at the *sanguinary* practice of Sir Astley. An anecdote connected with royalty, will serve as an apt illustration.

Sir Astley Cooper was the confidential physician of George the Fourth, and upon one occasion, when that monarch was afflicted with a serious malady that appeared to baffle the skill of Sir Astley and his co-physicians, the Duke of York, brother of the king, drove to the residence of Abernethy, in whose skill he had unlimited confidence. The Doctor's carriage was at the door, and the Doctor himself was about entering it, as the illustrious visitor arrived. Old Abernethy was no courtier, and he was as bluff as honesty itself. When informed of the object of the Duke's visit, he shook his head gruffly. "No, no," said he, "let him send for his butcher; I can't go, for I have my poor hospital patients to attend to, and I won't neglect them for all the kings in Christendom."

Here was a sample of democracy one would hardly expect to meet with in monarchical England.

There is no disputing the fact, that the knife is a source of immense mischief to the human family. Every day brings us tidings of some unfortunate man or woman being ushered into eternity through the means of a surgical operation. I could name twenty cases which have occurred within a year, when the persons were in a common degree of health at the time the operations for different purposes were commenced, and all of whom died in less than a week after undergoing such operations. How melancholy would the reflection be, if, from an absolute necessity, physicians were compelled to operate in this manner, and when the fact was known that such operations were generally followed by death. But what different feelings inspire us, when we reflect that most of those operations are undertaken and performed *without any necessity*, and only to exhibit to the world the manual surgical tact of a vaporing, iron-hearted M. D. That in nine cases out of ten, when operations are performed and death ensues, the patient might have been cured or sensibly benefited, we have not the shadow of a doubt. For, as Professor Abernethy says, "It is owing to our ignorance that the knife is used in any case."

Is it asked what will we substitute for mercury and the knife? we answer that, for mineral poisons, we substitute the vegetables that grow in Nature's garden; we have tried them, and we find them abundantly successful. Moreover, we find them of such variety in strength and medicinal qualities, as to answer every indication disease presents, and to accomplish all, and much more than the conjoined use of calomel and the lancet. Diseases which have been given up by mineral practitioners, have been cured by vegetable prescriptions, both here and elsewhere. A vast number of cases denominated surgical, in which deadly operations have been recommended, have been completely cured by the Reformed Practice. Indeed, in no department of God's vast scheme of goodness to man is that goodness so strikingly exhibited as in the arrangements of medicinal plants to restore health and remove obstinate diseases. All that is required of us is, to know the medicinal quantity of each plant and the disease it is designed to cure; then, when we are sick, we may put forth our hand and take it as the boon of Heaven.

It becomes our duty to investigate the quality of each plant, from the forest tree down to the humble ivy; and, in the performance of this duty, I trust that we have the prayers of the philanthropist and the patronage of every good man. It is a work of vast importance to the human family; and if we have found substitutes for minerals, the lancet, and the knife, surely the world will not withhold from us that respect or patronage which so great a discovery demands. Some physicians of the old school will jeer, and mock, and lie, and slander; but their efforts to put down our system will be in vain. The mass of the people are on our side; they are our defense, our judges, and rewarders. Beside, the object of our pursuit is, above all others, calculated to cheer us in our researches and comfort us in our privations, having no less object in view than the redemption of the rising generation from the evils of mineral poison and blood-letting, and our army, navy, and other unfortunate fellow-beings from the horrors of the scalpel and amputating-knife.

A system should consist of just, logical deductions, drawn from familiar, known, indubitable, and undoubted *facts*. Instead of this, all our systems are either false conclusions from mere imaginary whims, begged principles, or mere suppositions; or even false conclusions from erroneous principles. All systemizers pretend to build upon facts; but their facts are *pressed* and *whipped* into their service. The doctor first spins his system out of the cobweb of his fancy, and afterward squeezes some facts into forms resembling proofs of it, and very honestly shuts his eyes against all such facts as are at variance with his beloved air-castle. He creates distinctions, when in nature all is whole, and forges classifications, when in nature all swims together. Thus Boerhaave, Cullen, Brown, Darwin, Staehl, are all blind leaders of the blind; and the young physician, who thinks he has in his notes and books a remedy for every disease, when he comes to the sick-bed, finds all a chaos; no rule will apply: he looks in vain for the vaunted effects of his cure-all nostrums; forsakes in disgust a practice which may lead him to manslaughter, or from experience chalks himself out some dictionary:—This is good for that, or that is good for this, and becomes a *quack;* for practice without system is the very definition of quackery. Another, and not less efficient cause of the falsity of our medical systems is, the prejudiced respect for ancient and modern celebrated *names.* The most important data presented to us by modern improvements in physiology and anatomy (the marrow of the medical science) are bartered away for the *dicta* of Hippocrates, Galen, Boerhaave, Cullen, and Rush; and thus the lancet, or calomel, or cold-bath, or opium, or salt of tartar, all in their turn, become *panaceas* (cure-alls) with the accession of every new popular profession; and

"For the king's offense the people die."

I offer to the public a *new system of medical science,* which I have formed conscientiously clear of all those impediments, and which is confirmed in its salutary effects by the experience of a life-time's practice. •

Subjoined, are some pertinent views of Mr. Thomas Jefferson, who did not belong to the profession, but who, by-the-bye, possessed an extraordinary mind, and who was fully competent to judge correctly upon this subject:

We know, from what we see and feel, that the animal body is, in its organs and functions, subject to derangement, inducing pain and tending to its destruction. In this disordered state we observe nature providing for the re-establishment of order, by exciting some salutary evacuation of the morbilic matter, or by some other operation which escapes our imperfect senses and researches. She brings on a crisis by stools, vomiting, sweat, urine, expectoration, etc., which, for the most part, ends in the restoration of healthy action. Experience has taught us, also, that there are certain substances by which, applied to the living body, internally or externally, we can at will produce the same evacuations, and thus do in a short time what nature would do but slowly, and do effectually what perhaps she would not have strength to accomplish. Where, then, we have seen a disease characterized by specific signs or phenomena, and relieved by a certain *natural* evacuation or process, whenever that disease occurs under the same appearances, we may reasonably count on producing a solution of it, by the use of such substances as we have found, *by experience*, produce the same evacuation or movement. Thus, fullness of the stomach we can relieve by emetics; diseases of the bowels by purgatives, etc., etc. Here, then, the judicious, the moral, the humane physician should stop. * * * But the adventurous physician goes on, and substitutes presumption for knowledge. From the scanty field of what is known, he launches into the boundless regions of what is unknown. He establishes for his guide some fanciful theory of corpuscular attraction of chemical agency, of mechanical powers, of stimuli, of irritability accumulated or exhausted, of depletion by the lancet and repletion by mercury, or some other ingenious dream which lets him into all nature's secrets at short hand. On the principle which he thus assumes he forms his table of nosology, arrays his diseases into families, and extends his curative treatment (says he) by analogy, to all he has thus arbitrarily marshaled together.

I have lived myself to see the disciples of Hoffman, Boerhaave, Staehl, Cullen, and Brown succeed one another like the shifting figures of the magic lantern, and their fancies, like the dresses of the annual doll-babies from Paris, becoming, from their novelty, the vogue of the day, and yielding to the next novelty their ephemeral favors. The patient, treated on the *fashionable* theory, sometimes gets well in spite of the medicine. The medicine, therefore, restored him, and the young doctor receives new courage to proceed in his bold experiments on the lives of his fellow-creatures.

I believe we may safely affirm that the *inexperienced* and *presumptuous* band of medical tyros let loose upon the world, *destroys more human life* in one year than all the Robin Hoods, Cartouches, and Macheaths do in a century.

It is in this part of medicine I wish to see a reform, an abandonment of hypothesis for sober *facts*—the *first* degree of value set on *clinical observation*, and the *lowest* on *visionary theories*. I would wish the young practitioner, especially, to have deeply impressed on his mind the real limits of his art.   .*   *   *   *

The *only* sure foundations of medicine are an intimate knowledge of the human body, and *observation* of the effects of medicinal substances on that. The anatomical and clinical schools, therefore, are those in which the young physician should be formed. If he enters, with innocence, that of the *theory* of medicine, it is scarcely *possible* that he should come out *untainted* with *error*. His mind must be strong indeed, if, rising above juvenile credulity, he can maintain a wise infidelity against the authority of his instructors and the bewitching delusion of their theories. * * * * I hope and believe that it is from this side of the Atlantic that Europe, which has taught us so many other things, will be led into sound principles in this branch of science, the most important of all others being that to which we commit the care of health and life. (*Letter to Dr. Wister*, vol. iv, page 91.)

There is no science that has so much needed reform as the science of medicine, for it is a science in which the happiness of mankind is more closely woven than any other. All reformers have to struggle with prejudice and superstition, but none so much as the hardy individual who dare attack the quackery and humbug of the old-time medical practitioner. In some sensible and well-timed remarks of Dr. A. R. Porter, addressed to the *Botanic Medical Reformer*, I find the following:

The world needs to go through a process of purification, in order to make it what it ought to be, and I shall always feel proud to lend a helping hand to carry on the noble enterprise. But as it is impossible to do every thing at once, those which stand out most prominently deserve our immediate attention; and upon such should be unhesitatingly directed the weapons of reform.

Among these conspicuous evils there is one on which I have bestowed no little consideration. It is the present practice of medicine. Medical Reform—that is the question. It is in the common, or regular system of practice, so called, that I desire to see a thorough radical reform. If I could be fully persuaded in my own mind that the use of poisonous mineral ingredients, such as mercury, antimony, arsenic, and the like, are safe, sure, and efficacious remedies, and did not produce effects deleterious to the human constitution; if I were assured that there were no substitutes to be found in nature's extensive vegetable dispensary more admirably adapted to the nature of disease, and which could not cure without making the last state worse than the first, I certainly would abandon my idea of a reform, and cheerfully submit to the present system, and risk my life and health altogether upon its own merits.

But while I am fully convinced, from observation and experience, that the regular practice of medicine is absolutely imperfect and highly dangerous; and while I am satisfied that the vegetable system of practice, which is now extending itself rapidly over the Western portion of our country, is eminently superior to every other with which our land is superabundantly stocked, I can not too anxiously desire a reform. It is on this subject that I wish the people to be aroused to proper and honorable action.

It is time that this apathy and indifference, which has existed in the minds of the mass of the people on the subject of medicine, and which is totally at variance with its great importance, should be totally removed; for there is surely no art or science of so much consequence to their well-being as that which has for its object the preservation of health and the cure of disease.

As there are but few tried, faithful, sterling advocates (comparatively speaking) of the vegetable system of practice in this country, it may seem presumptuous to undertake so great an enterprise, while a powerful monopoly, propped up by public opinion, hemmed in by constitutional barriers, combining genius and wit, learning and talent, are bending all their mighty energies against us. But I hope that an intelligent people will not be daunted by this; for the more the reformed practice becomes known, the more the people will appreciate and support it.

The practice of medicine should be divested of all those *technicalities* which the most limited intellect can not clearly understand. It should be based upon true, scientific, philosophical principles, employing such remedies as will act in perfect harmony with the laws of nature and animal life.

The grand mystery to be understood in the practice of medicine is, not to create disease, but to remove it; and as disease is obstruction, such medicines as will assist nature in removing obstruction are the only remedial agents that can be safely and successfully employed.

Where, then, the question is asked, are these remedial agents to be obtained? Not in the submarine depths of the Atlantic or the Pacific, nor in the impenetrable regions of the terraqueous globe; but in the vegetable kingdom, in the little plant that shoots heavenward its spiral boughs, and spreads out its tinsel leaves to receive the drops of the silver dew or the warm beams of the noonday sun.

In the vegetable kingdom there may be found the elixir of health; there may be found the healing balm. Would to Heaven that the study of this extensive division of natural objects was more generally pursued and appreciated. Because, if it were, and the medicinal properties of plants better understood, disease might be more easily and successfully treated.

In the vegetable kingdom an All-wise Being has deposited such plants and herbs as are congenial to our constitutions, and adapted to the cure of all curable diseases to which human nature is incident. We have no need, then, to resort to the application of poisonous mineral ingredients (such as mercury and the like) in the cure of disease, because they do not answer the purpose of their application; they clog up the system and poison the fountains of life, and make the patient a sickly, wretched being through the remainder of his days. I appeal to the lame, the sick, and the blind; to the toothless and deformed; to the dyspeptic, the hypochondriac; to the individual of scrofulous habit and ulcerated gums; to the rheumatic invalid and broken-down constitution, who are the unhappy victims of mercurial empiricism. It is a lamentable fact, that the most active and potent articles used by the faculty as medicines, and upon which they place their principal reliance, are destructive to life and injurious to health, the latter of which they are intended to promote.

But many there are, I know, who will not believe it. Intelligent and well-meaning as they may be, their prejudices have become so deep-rooted in favor of the mineral practice, that it is almost impossible to turn their attention to the work of reform.

There are many, too, who are capable of discriminating between a true and false system of medicine, who are almost prepared to go for a thorough reform, but can not abandon altogether the use of minerals, because they think that calomel, blue pill, or some other preparation of mercury is indispensably necessary to the cure of diseased liver. But however strongly inclined they may be to this opinion, it is, nevertheless erroneous. Calomel may exert a potent, powerful action on the liver, and give it mere temporary relief. By its acrid and irritating nature, it arouses it to action; the secretion of bile is increased, the bowels are moved, and the patient feels relieved; but this relief is of short duration; in a few weeks he finds his liver has become torpid, and even more inactive than before, and he again has recourse to another dose, with the same results as before; and thus he continues to take dose after dose, until the healthy tone of his stomach and bowels is irrecoverably gone, and by and by falls a victim to the combined agency of his original disease and the deadly remedy which he took for the purpose of removing it. In confirmation of what I have said, I will give the opinion of Dr. Barnwell. He says: " Mercury will produce the liver complaint." Dr. Hamilton and Dr. Fies state " that it will in, some constitutions, lie inert for years, and then burst forth with tremendous violence; and that it destroys the digestive organs." Dr. Hamilton also declares " that every physician of competent knowledge does know these deadly effects of mercury on the constitution."

I am acquainted with an individual who has been afflicted with liver complaint for a number of years, who has been in the habit of taking a dose of calomel every time he felt the alarming symptoms, but without any positive cure. And I know another individual who has had the same disease a much longer time than the former, and equally as formidable, who has entirely cured himself by the use of vegetable medicines.

Of the superiority of vegetable over mineral medicines, I can fully testify from my own individual experience and observation, having witnessed some of the most astonishing cures performed by their application. Of the effects of the latter I speak with pain, living to see a near friend dragging out a miserable life, produced by the administration of poisonous mineral drugs.

In view of the evils of the present system of medicine, a reformation is loudly called for; something more safe and effectual must be had; and I trust that it will go on, until the glaring inconsistencies in the healing art are ferreted out and held up to the indignation of an injured community, and the vegetable system of practice substituted to meet the emergencies of the people.

OUR MOTTO.

We use such balms as have no strife
With Nature or the laws of Life;
With blood our hands we never stain,
Nor poison men to ease their pain.

Our Father—whom all goodness fills,
Provides the means to cure all ills;
The simple herbs beneath our feet.
Well used, relieve our pains complete.

A simple herb, a simple flower,
    Culled from the dewy lea—
These, these shall speak with touching power
    Of change and health to thee.

                        F. TUMBLETY, M. D.

Although no great admirer of Barnum, I nevertheless regard him as a great authority in the matter of successfully conducting a business, and he himself considers advertising as the great element of his success. Indeed, there is an anecdote that was told me by a gentleman who advertised an exhibition with which he was connected some years ago, strongly illustrative of this. It was in Chicago, and all the papers, save one, came out with whole column advertisements nearly two weeks before the advent of the "show."

In the mean time Barnum arrived in the city, and the next morning had all the morning papers brought to his room, including the one in which his agent had omitted to advertise.

" How is it," inquired the great showman, " that there is no notice or advertisement in this journal ?"

" Oh," replied the agent, " I was informed that it is an old fossilated Whig paper, supported by the contributions of some of the time-honored members, out of consideration for the editor, who has been an old wheel-horse of the party. Indeed, I am assured that the daily edition does not exceed three hundred."

" Three hundred," repeated Barnum. " Let me see; three sixes are eighteen—that is, upon an average computation, each paper is read by six people, which makes eighteen hundred daily. This is worth seeing to, so you had better go at once and tell the publisher to copy the advertisement;" and sure enough the next morning out came the advertisement, and a complimentary notice beside, which latter Barnum cut out and put into his scrap-book; for my informant adds, that no man he ever knew was so sensitive to the good or evil report of the press, as this celebrated caterer for the amusement of the public.

Now, I know that there is a vast amount of humbuggery in the advertising market; but I am also aware, as every sensible observer must be, that no matter how beneficial or excellent, no article can be fairly presented to the public without the aid of the press, and to this end advertising is the only medium. Hence, in the course of my professional career, I have deemed it a duty to myself and the public to advertise, and I have done so extensively. I believe that

I have, in this manner, patronized newspapers to an amount exceeding ninety thousand dollars, and herein, by precept and example, I may be said to deserve well of the press, to whom I have never been indebted to the amount of a dollar. Indeed, I can affirm that, to my knowledge, I do not owe a single individual either in or out of the press, and to substantiate this, I am prepared to present any one with a thousand dollars who can bring me an account that I have left unsettled.

I have alluded to the great injury to my health from the incarceration, privation, and horror I experienced in the Washington bastile, better known as the "Old Capitol Prison." Compensation for this is beyond all price, for health is an inestimable jewel that can not be purchased with gold; and I feel that I shall never again realize the hardy and robust *physique* for which I was distinguished previous to my arrest in St. Louis. But the pecuniary loss I have sustained, and the disarrangement of my business, are other matters, for which I have a clear claim upon a government by whose authority I have been so outraged and despoiled. I will here just adduce one instance as a sample, and it will be seen how my professional reputation has been trifled and tampered with.

Upon my return to the West, and while laying over in Indianapolis, I was waited upon by a person of genteel address and consummate impudence, which latter will be pretty well exemplified by the following:

He introduced himself as from Louisville, and hearing of my arrival in Indianapolis, he said that he had come to pay me a visit.

I acknowledged the compliment, and, at the same

time, I desired to know why I was indebted for this honor.

"Oh, Doctor," said he, "I 'll tell you all in good time. You see, I heard of your arrest in St. Louis, and how you were whisked off to Washington, that celebrated

"'——— bourne
From whence no traveler returns;'

at least I thought so, in the case of gentlemen who, like yourself, were snapped up by order of the all-per-vading Edwin Stanton. However, you are an excep-tion, for which you may thank your lucky star, which, somehow or other, must have been largely in the ascendant."

"Well, sir," I remarked, "I know all this, and now for the especial occasion to which I am indebted for this visit."

"All in good time," replied my free-and-easy ac-quaintance, "all in good time, for I am coming at once to the point. You see, that hearing, as I have remarked, of your arrest, and knowing the great repu-tation you have acquired as the Indian Herb Doctor, I thought it a pity that such first-rate capital should be lost to the world; and, moreover, being under the impression that, in consequence of your having got into Stanton's clutches, the aforesaid world, in an outer point of view, had looked its last upon you, I deter-mined to step into your shoes, which I did, and as you will fully concede, to pretty good purpose."

"What, sir," said I, with a perceptible flush of in-dignation, "do you mean to say that you have been personating me?"

"Keep cool," replied my imperturbable visitor, "for

4

I intend to be candid with you, if only for the gratitude I owe for the use of your title. I have told you
truly that I never expected you would revisit the
outer world, professionally or otherwise, and hence I
deemed that it would n't be the slightest injury to you,
my going to some place where you have not practiced,
and taking your title of the Indian Herb Doctor. I
found out that you had never been to Louisville, but
it did n't take long after my arrival there, to discover
that your name and fame were not strange to that
community. In short, I played my *role* with such success, that I soon had more practice than I could attend
to; but," he added, laughing, "I am afraid that I did
not advance your reputation in the Falls City, for,
honestly, I believe that I have about played myself
out; however, I made hay while the sun shone, and
here is the result "—unfolding a pocket-book, and taking
out a draft for $8,000—"which I have made clear in
the course of my short practice."

I was dumb with astonishment at the cool impudence of the fellow, and indignation at the trick he
had played upon the public in my name, when, finding
that I did not speak, he went on:

"And now, Dr. Tumblety, I come to the practical
and business portion of my visit. As I have said, I
have made this $8,000 in a manner under false pre-
tenses, by taking your title. You are again free—
something I did not expect—and doubtless prepared
to resume your profession and standing. Now, I offer
you this eight thousand dollars, upon condition that
you take me under your instructions—now, then, say,
is it a bargain?"

I must have been poor indeed to have accepted this

offer; so, telling him that I regarded him as the most unblushing impostor that had thus far ever crossed my path, I pointed to the door, a gesture which he at once comprehended. Nevertheless, he walked toward it with the most provoking composure, bowed with admirable *sang-froid*, and disappeared, since which I have never seen his face.

I have already alluded to a resolution taken upon the breaking out of the civil war, of tendering my professional services to the Government, in which event I should have received an appointment on the medical staff. This I subsequently abandoned, in consequence of ill health, but it seems that the report had reached my relatives in Europe that I was attached to the United States Army, as also that I had fallen in one of the engagements. I first knew this by meeting with Captain Anderson, of the royal navy, but extensively and favorably known in this country, wherein he made himself a legion of friends, as the commander of the steamship Great Eastern.

He knew me well, as also my relatives, a long time previous, while he was the captain of one of the Cunard line of packets, and while I resided in Boston, at the time the steamers came to that port. He frequently pressed me to take a trip with him to Europe, to visit my friends there, among whom I had a near relative and namesake, Tumblety, who has been connected over twenty years with the Cunard line. On one of his trips the Captain took my daguerreotype to my uncle in England, who has since died, in order to satisfy him that I was still in the land of the living.

Another distinguished commander in the Cunard

line, Captain Moody, was also an intimate friend of my family, and he, too, I used to meet with friendly greeting, at the old Tremont, in Boston. I recall these reunions with pleasurable emotion, for they were magnetic links that connected me with dear friends far away across the stormy Atlantic. Nevertheless, it is not for the purpose of indulging pleasant reminiscences that I have introduced these personages, but simply in proof of my standing in society, for the many friends and acquaintances of Captain Anderson will understand that the person he would take by the hand must command a spotless character and a gentlemanly record.

I can not trust myself to reflect upon the cruel manner in which I have been treated, and the indignity I have suffered; for at such times I feel the hot blood tingling to my finger ends, and it requires a strong effort to calm an indignation which, if allowed full scope, might lead the victim of a tyrannical despot to contemplate redress, by personal chastisement upon the author of his misfortunes. Thank Heaven, there is considerable philosophy in my composition, and I can bear and forbear, or, at least, bide my time.

> " For time at last sets all things even—
> And if we do but watch the hour,
> There never yet was human power,
> Which could evade, if unforgiven,
> The patient search and vigil long
> Of him who treasures up a wrong."

I certainly have been fortunate in the majority of my acquaintance, and it has moreover consisted, in a great measure, of those whose association should have been sufficient to vouch for my loyalty to the Government. In the category I take pride in recalling the name of General Joe Hooker, with whom I have, for a long period, been upon terms of cordial friendship. I met him last summer at Saratoga, and was happy to experience proof of his continued kindly feeling by his cordial recognition. At the same fashionable place of resort, I met Lieutenant-General Grant, to whom I was introduced, and by whom I was treated with flattering consideration. Certainly my character could not be more satisfactorily sustained, than in the recognition of two such illustrious men and distinguished warriors.

In a previous portion of this sketch, there is mention of a distribution of flour to the poor of Buffalo. I will here add, that it is my usual custom to remember the needy of every city in which I practice, and my method of benefiting them is to my mind the most practical. I know that bogus benevolence exists to a lamentable extent in every community, and I have had experience how mercenary and designing persons, under the hollow pretense of collecting funds for charitable purposes, impose upon the public, and appropriate the funds so raised, or at least the greater portion of them, to their own use. While, therefore, I am constantly importuned by such persons to contribute to their peculiar charities, I seldom respond; at the same time I challenge the world to prove that any legitimate claimant ever left my threshold empty-handed. My distribution of flour was not in an ostentatious spirit, but simply as a means to benefit, in a small way, the largest number of the suffering poor within my means. I do not court fame, for with Col-

ton, of present fame I think little, and of the future,
less; for the praises we receive after we are buried,
like the flowers that are strewed over our grave, may
be gratifying to the living, but they are nothing to the
dead; the dead are gone, either to the place where they
hear them not, or where, if they do, they will despise
them. No, I do not covet fame for my alms, but if
I can leave behind me a name and reputation as an
alleviator of the bodily ills that afflict poor humanity, my mission upon earth will be accomplished.

Since, however, I have tasted of the hospitality of
the Old Capitol Prison, there is another class of suf-
ferers with whom I would share my last crust. I
mean the poor victims of Stanton, that same Edwin
before whose tyranny the acts that cost Charles the
First his head are tame and trivial. And, *aporopos*,
I am here reminded of an article I clipped from the
Cincinnati *Commercial*, a Republican journal, from its
Washington correspondent. Here it is:

> I trust this Congress will do something to settle the question
> whether the Government under which we live is a republic, of which
> Andrew Johnson is President, with Edwin M. Stanton—to use the
> language of a distinguished military chieftain—"a d — d clerk,"
> or whether it is really an absolute monarchy, under the reign of
> Edwin I. Pope's couplet, about forms of government, may be all
> very well enough for philosophy, but it won't do for actual practice,
> after all. If Edwin is really king, by all means let him have the
> crown and the name. As to his authority, there is no need of change
> in that, for what he exercises now is limitless, and what is limitless
> can't be extended—so the mathematicians say, and they're right.
> But if Edwin is not actually king, then it would pay to inquire by
> what authority he arrested and sent to prison a reporter of a Wash-
> ington paper within a week, for publishing a harmless item of news;
> and by what authority he denies the use of the telegraph wires to
> the conductors of loyal newspapers in the South, while he permits

gamblers, speculators, and prostitutes to use them, *ab libitum*. If he has a right to say that such and such matter shall not go to the New Orleans papers by telegraph, has n't he a right to say it shall not go by mail, and therefore a right to interdict the transmission of Northern papers through the mail to the South, and for that matter, to stop the mails entirely? Where does power leave off an l usurpation begin, with the autocrat of the War Department? Or can there be such a thing as usurpation by kings? Is it "loyal" to ask the question? Think of a d—d clerk of the President's having a mounted guard stationed in front of his palace day and night to prevent carriages from driving past and raising a dust to permeate his highness' chambers, and perchance reach the royal nostrils; and a guard of honor at the hall door, too! The reader may be incredulous, but it 's an actual fact that for months past no public or private conveyance has been allowed to drive past the residence of Edwin I, and the preventing power has been a couple of United States Cavalry soldiers. What a glorious occupation for the volunteer army—keeping the dust out of Mr. Stanton's window curtains! Who would n't rush to arms for such a glorious purpose? Who 'd hesitate? None but an arrant Copperhead. Happy Edwin, in the possession of a dust guard; but thrice happy guard in such a post of honor!

"As the tree is known by its fruit," so are the works of a good physician proven by the evidence of those who have been benefited by his treatment. With this view, I select only a portion of the multitude of certificates that have been voluntarily furnished me.

TESTIMONIALS.

THE undersigned, citizens and residents of Toronto, U. C., hereby certify that we have known Dr. Tumblety, the Indian Herb Doctor, for a long time; we consider him a gentleman in every sense of the word. He enjoys the reputation of being skilled in the art of healing the sick by means exceedingly simple and effective. He has been extensively patronized, and many of his patients speak very highly of his ability in the practice of his profession:

T. W. Teevin, Professor of Penmanship.
Thos. Barry, Solicitor, York Chambers.
William Reford, Grocer, Market Square.
Michael McDowd, Contractor, Duchess Street
P. Doyle, Bookseller, Arcade.
P. O'Neil, Grocer.
George Platt, Albion Hotel.
William J. Dugdale, Grocer, Nelson Street.
James W. Trotter.
J. Briggs, Broker, Geryard Street.
P. J. O'Neil, Wholesale Dry Goods, Yonge Street.
James Matthews, Proprietor International Hotel.
W. Beaty, Wholesale Boots and Shoes, 62½ King Street.
Charles Moore, Grocer, Yonge Street.
Patrick Daly, Merchant, Yonge Street,
Joseph B. Quinn, Hotel Keeper, Market Square.
R. P. Crooks, Alderman.
H. Sproat, Councilman.
Daniel Devlin, Merchant, Queen Street.
J. A. Donovan, Law Student.
George Brownlee, Manager of Cleveland's Printing Office, Yonge
　　Street.

Merrick & Bros., Drapers, King Street.

James Cropper, Gas-fitting Establishment, 182 King Street.

H. P. Dwight, Superintendent Montreal Telegraph Co.

William Jackson, Adelaide Street.

Alex. Jacques, }
F. M. Farrel, } Proprietors of " Merchants' Press."

William Windeat, Artist, 3 King Street.

Robert Reford, Grocer.

T. W. McConkey, Hotel Keeper, King Street.

H. Jones Smith, Foundryman, Bathurst Street.

Mark Ackerman, Dining Saloon, Wellington Street.

L. Oliver, Land Agent, Church Street.

C. V. Archibald, Accountant, Park Street.

Joseph Carson, Arcade.

William Dover, 18 Arcade.

J. McDonald, }
D. D. Forest, } British and American Express Co.
D. McCarthy, }

C. H. Sheppard, Accountant.

Richard Couch, Architect, Adelaide Street.

John Blackburn, Proprietor of " City Steam Press," Yonge Street.

Alex. Urquhart, Surgeon, Yonge Street.

John O'Gorman, Jeweler, Yonge Street.

J. P. Carson, Daguerrean Artist, corner of King and Yonge Street.

John Dixon, Auctioneer, Yorkville.

William Granger, 4 Arcade.

Henry D. Duncan, Painter and Glazier, Louis Street.

John Walsh, King Street.

John H. Lyon, Tragedian, Richmond Street.

William Schluchter, Editor and Proprietor of the German *Observer*.

Louis Kurth, Hotel Keeper.

George Mathias, Optician.

S. Mansfield, Merchant.

I have known Dr. Francis Tumblety since he came to Toronto. I have always found him a gentleman, and as such, will ever respect him.

I also believe him to be a man skilled in his profession, for I know of several cases in this vicinity (one in my own family) which had

been given up as hopeless by the Faculty, but were cured by his
remedies.   JAMES TAYLOR,
    October 15, 1857.   *J. P., Township of York, C. W.*

[*From the Brantford Christian Messenger.*]

DR. TUMBLETY, THE INDIAN HERB DOCTOR.—Not long since we
alluded to the wonderful cures effected by this gentleman, at and
around Hamilton and London, of which the *Spectator, Banner, Christian Advocate, Free Press*, and *Atlas* speak in the most laudatory
terms. In another column of to-day's issue, under the heading of
"Special Notice," will be found authenticated certificates from individuals respecting the benefit they have derived from Dr. Tumblety's
medicines. We have in our possession a large number of similar
certificates, but have omitted to insert them, being persuaded that
those which we have given to-day sufficiently demonstrate that
gentleman's skill and success in the treatment of disease. We are
glad to know that he bids fair to be equally successful in Brantford.
Crowds of people are resorting to him for advice, and many are already experiencing considerable relief from taking his medicines.
Nearly every disease to which the human system is subject seems
to give way under Dr. Tumblety's treatment, and to which the following lines appear applicable:

> The deaf shall hear, the trembling limb be strong,
> And groans of anguish mellow into song;
> The infant, moaning on his mother's breast,
> Shall fondly play, or smiling sink to rest.

QUEBEC.

[*From the Quebec Morning Chronicle.*]

The cure of Mr. Poulin we consider one of the most miraculous
wonders in the world, which Dr. Tumblety has accomplished. We
are personally acquainted with Mr. Poulin, and saw him when he
was suffering, and again saw him in our office yesterday, well.

                                    QUEBEC, *June* 21, 1858.

This is to certify that I have been suffering from Epileptic Fits
for a long time; after trying Dr. Robitaille, Dr. Malcolm, and Dr.
Nault, without receiving the least particle of relief from these medical gentlemen. Reader, just think of dying two or three times a

day, and you can form an idea of my sufferings. I was at the very point of death when I commenced using Dr. Tumblety's medicine, and I had not the slightest hope of recovery. But, strange to say, I have not had a single fit since I put myself under Dr. Tumblety's care.

MAURICE POULIN.

[*Sworn to before His Worship, George Hall, Esq., Mayor of Quebec.*]

QUEBEC, *June* 13, 1857.

This is to certify that I have been blind for ten years of my right eye, and for the last ten months my left eye became similarly diseased. Four weeks ago I was led by three members of the St. Patrick's Society into Dr. Tumblety's office, almost blind ; the Doctor, after examining me, said he could cure me in a short time, notwithstanding most of the doctors in town gave me up as incurable, viz. : Dr. Landry, and Dr. Fremont of the Nunnery Hospital ; they gave me up after thirteen weeks' treatment, and my wife led me home blind from the institution. Then I commenced trying mostly all the doctors of Quebec, without the slightest particle of relief. I have been to work for the last eight or ten days at my usual occupation, that of a pilot on the St. Lawrence. Thanks to the Almighty God, that he has sent the illustrious Dr. Tumblety to cure me. May God bless him.

WILLIAM SMITH,
Citizen of Quebec, C. E.

Sworn to and acknowledged by the above-mentioned Wm. Smith, who has read aloud in my presence a printed document which he had never seen before.

GEORGE HALL,
Acting Mayor of Quebec.

L. O'Brien's son, cured of consumption. Sworn to before D. B. Galbraith, J. P., of Hamilton, this fifth day of August, 1856.

John Magee, cured of scurvy, Bathurst Street, London, C. W. Sworn to before me, this eleventh day of April, 1856.

WILLIAM BARKER,
Mayor of London, C. W.

Thomas Coke, cured of paralysis, township of Binbrook, C. W.

Remarkable Cure of Cancer.

ANCASTER, *August* 16, 1856.

DR. F. TUMBLETY:

Dear Sir—This is to certify that I had a cancer on my lip for nineteen months. I spent much time and money in the use of the most popular medicines, and the practice of physicians, but of no avail. I was told my case was hopeless. My head and lip were dreadfully painful, and this was my condition when I was persuaded to try your unparalleled skill. I did so, and before using two bottles of your medicine I began to get relief; the cancer and inflammation began to subside as I continued its use, and I am happy to say I am perfectly cured. Yours truly, ELIZA DUFFY.

Sworn before me, at Hamilton, this sixteenth day of August, 1856.

D. B. GALBRAITH, J. P.

[*Sworn before His Worship the Mayor of Toronto, J. Hutchinson, Esq.*]

The extraordinary history of that philanthropic and charitable physician, the Indian Herb Doctor, F. Tumblety, of No. 111 King Street East, Toronto, C. W., should be engraved on adamant.

Last summer I was so unfortunate as to fall and injure my leg, which pained me a little at the time, but soon passed away. About five weeks after, the pain, accompanied with a swelling, returned—slightly at first, but continued growing worse, till I was confined to my bed. The best physicians of Toronto were called in and their prescriptions used, but no relief could be obtained. At last I was given up by them; one of them said I was in the last stage of galloping consumption, and could never recover. The pains I suffered were so intense that for weeks together I could neither sleep nor obtain any rest. I became so weakened that I often fainted, and sometimes I would have two or three fits before consciousness would return.

This was my apparently helpless condition when I applied to the Indian Herb Doctor, F. Tumblety. Under his skillful treatment I was free from pain in two days, and continued gradually to improve. Thanks to his unremitting and assiduous care, I am now restored to perfect health. CHARLOTTE I. REYNOLDS, *King St. East.*

Sworn before me, this ninth day of February, 1857.

JOHN HUTCHINSON, *Mayor of Toronto.*

We, the undersigned, are witnesses to the facts and cure of Miss Reynolds:

H. P. Dwight, Supt. Mon. Telegraph.

W. Brown, Yonge Street.

T. Green, ⎫
J. W. T. Green, ⎬ Green Bros
W. V. Dossor, King Street.

H. Smith, King Street.

Mrs. Col. Savage.

The Misses Savage.

W. Savage, late Col. Royal Artillery.

Charles Medforth, cured of consumption, pain in the breast, spitting blood, palpitation of the heart. References: A. Dickey & Co., Soho Foundry, John Taylor & Bros.

Mrs. Carret, cured of blindness.

Mr. Brennan, cured of scurvy.

MONTREAL.

MONTREAL, *Dec.* 7, 1857.

This is to certify that I have been afflicted with typhus fever four weeks. Having been reduced to very great feebleness, I began to discover the alarming symptoms of death, and my physicians told me that they could do no more for me. I was recommended by some of my friends to send for Dr. Tumblety. I did so, and the effect of his medicines on my worn and diseased system was like magic. I am now enjoying such health as I have not known for years, and I have been at my work at Mr. Brash's Foundry, King Street, Griffintown, this last three weeks. AUGUST MAESER,
Nazareth St., Griffintown.

Sworn before me, this eighth day of December, 1857.

HENRY STARNES, *Mayor.*

MONTREAL, *Dec.* 7, 1857.

This is to certify that I have been afflicted with cancer on my lip for upward of two years, which the doctors of the city failed to cure, till I applied to Dr. Tumblety, who has cured me of it in six days. It is now about one year since I applied to Dr. Reddy, and he told me that it was a slow cancer. Dr. McDonald told me it would have to be cut out, and that it might cause my death; therefore I applied to Dr. Tumblety, who has cured me and saved my life. ELLEN FAGAN.

Sworn before me, this eighth day of December, 1857.

HENRY STARNES, *Mayor.*

Joseph Craig, cured of bad cough, weakness, and debility, 47 Jure Street.

Mrs. Mary Keough, cured of palpitation of the heart, Wellington Street.

Mrs. McGibbon, cured of weakness, 6 Berthelet Street.

William Claudman, cured of chronic rheumatism and paralysis, with great debility, Hotel Keeper, 156 St. Mary's Street.

Catharine Murphy, cured of dyspepsia, Ottawa Hotel, Great St. James's Street.

Francis Flynn, cured of consumption, 85 Gabriel Street.

Mrs. Mackenzie, cured of palpitation of the heart, severe cough, pain in the head, 137 Dorchester Street.

HAMILTON, *July* 18, 1856.

INDIAN HERB DOCTOR, F. TUMBLETY:

Dear Sir: Allow me to express my heartfelt gratitude to you for the miraculous cure performed on me. I know of no way by which I can sufficiently recompense you for having taken me from the margin of the grave and restored me to perfect health, contrary to my own expectations, those of my friends, and to every appearance, contrary to the very laws of nature. I was reduced to a mere skeleton from a disease peculiar to my sex; I had used most of the popular medicines in vain. I consulted with some six or seven physicians, and tried their remedies to no purpose, when I was recommended to try the Indian Herb Doctor, F. Tumblety, at the Burlington Hotel, Hamilton. I am thankful that I am able to assert to you and the world, that I am restored to perfect health, in a very few weeks.

These are facts; appropriate them as you think fit. I would merely suggest that you lay them before the public, that others may have the opportunity of doing likewise.

Respectfully, to serve the cause of humanity, etc.

MISS B. READY
Rebecca Street, Hamilton.

Sworn before me, this nineteenth day of July, 1856.

J. CUMMINGS, *Mayor.*

WASHINGTON.

The following testimonials are from well-known citizens of Washington, and they speak louder than any thing we could say. It is with pleasure we lay them before a candid and appreciative public. Our people are tired of theories. When a man is sick he wants the physician who prescribes remedies that are sure to cure him, and such a person is found in Dr. Tumblety, Indian Herb Doctor.— *Washington Star.*

Consumption Cured in the last stage.

WASHINGTON, *March* 14, 1862.

INDIAN HERB DOCTOR, F. TUMBLETY, M. D.:

Dear Sir: Supposing that others afflicted as I have been may be benefited by the knowledge and use of your remedies and treatment, I am induced to make the following statement:

For a long time I have been afflicted with consumption, said to be in the last stage, by many of the doctors in Washington and the District of Columbia. They all failed to cure me.

I applied to Dr. Tumblety, the Indian Herb Doctor. My coughing, spitting blood, pain in chest, are all gone, and have been for some time. My voice is quite restored. I feel as strong as ever, and from having been reduced to a skeleton, now weigh one hundred and thirty-two pounds.

As I experienced so much benefit from the use of Dr. Tumblety's medicines, I feel as though I could not say enough in their favor. Still, I feel thankful to God, the author and preserver of my life, that he has guided me to Dr. Tumblety, who has cured me.

JOHN A. LAIRD,
U. S. Capitol.

MAYOR'S OFFICE, WASHINGTON, *March* 18, 1862.

On this eighteenth day of March, 1862, personally appeared before me, William T. Dove, Acting Mayor of the City of Washington, John A. Laird, and made oath to the truth of said statement.

WILLIAM T. DOVE,
Acting Mayor.

Thomas Griffin, pains in the chest, back, shoulders, side, and head, accompanied with great debility and a melancholy and gloomy state of mind; cured. P Street, between Fifteenth and Sixteenth.

Mrs. Emma Kernall, erysipelas; cured. Fairfax Co., Virginia.

James H. Beall, cough, pain in the breast, dyspepsia, with great weakness; cured. Blacksmith-shop, Navy-yard.

Charles W. Harman, dyspepsia and liver complaint; cured. Metropolitan Police.

S. C. Parrish, ulcerated sore leg, with seven holes; cured. Seventh Street Park Hotel.

Mrs. Edward T. Tupipett, consumption; cured. Navy-yard, Third Street, between M and N.

James W. Larkin, very bad state of scurvy; cured. Government Printing-office.

Mrs. C. W. Blakeman, female complaint; cured. Lang's Hotel, Georgetown, D. C.

J. Maloney, scrofula; cured. Corner of Fourth and H Streets.

Frederick Rholeder, nervous debility; cured. F Street corner Second.

P. Downs, enlargement of the heart. 343 Sixth Street.

J. D. Lakeman, scrofula; cured. 439 Sixth Street.

Consumption cured: John Clark, Camp Duncan, D. C. · John C. Day, corner Second and O Streets.

John Herd, jaundice; cured. 500 New York Avenue.

David Dillon, fits; cured. 472 F Street.

John Donahu, nervous debility; cured. Corner C and Third Streets. Also Charles A. Courveiser, Navy-yard.

Cured of Chronic Disease: William Sullivan, corner of Four-and-a-half and G Streets, Iron Foundry, Navy-yard.

Charles Wilson, debility; cured. U. S. Regulars.

Benjamin Dorsey, dyspepsia; cured. Twentieth Street, below Pennsylvania Avenue.

James Reed, pimples on the face; cured. Twenty-sixth and L Streets.

M. G. Howard, chronic rheumatism; cured. Tenth Street, near Penn. Avenue.

S. J. White, asthma; cured. 253 B Street, south side of Capitol.

J. Blackburn, cancer; cured. Georgetown.

R. Haunseh, bad dreams, with night-sweats; cured. 417 Seventh Street.

Mrs. W. Tucker, disease peculiar to her sex; cured. Alexandria, Virginia.

Joseph Eskridge, consumption; cured. Brigade Wagon-master, Nineteenth Street.

Francis Scala, disease of the throat; cured. Leader of the U. S. Marine Band Navy-yard.

J. E. Hutchinson, scrofula; cured. Patent-office.

Rev. J. Curtis, dyspepsia and general debility; cured. Baltimore, Maryland.

Mrs. C. Capin, cancer; cured. Near Fairfax Seminary, Virginia.

P. Maher, sore eyes; cured. Bridge Street, Navy-yard.

Mrs. Capt. Cunningham, prolapsus uteri; cured. Georgetown, D. C.

James Davis, fits, weakness, dyspepsia, costiveness, night dreams; cured. Alexandria, Virginia.

James King, large tumor removed from the head, without the use of the knife. G Street.

BOSTON AND VICINITY.

UNIVERSITY PRESS, CAMBRIDGE, *May* 5.

DR. F. TUMBLETY:

Dear Sir—Supposing that others afflicted as I have been may be benefited by the knowledge and use of your remedies and treatment, I am induced to write you this communication.

For a number of years I had been afflicted with what I supposed to be a disease of the blood. The circulation of the blood seemed to be slow and obstructed in some way; my digestion was very imperfect. I was nervous and despondent, and troubled with headache very much, and had turns of sinking, faint, prostrate feelings, which were distressing, and alarmed me. Having tried numerous doctors without any benefit, I was advised by a friend to call upon you. I am now nearly restored to my former good health by the aid of your remedies.

I would most certainly recommend your treatment to any who may have been afflicted as I have been. Very truly yours,

A. K. P. WELCH.

A. Prince, scrofulous humor on the leg; cured. 149 Washington Street.

Son of D. H. Thorp, consumption; cured. Foreman of Boston Faucet Co.

Captain Luke's wife, prolapsus uteri; cured. 153 Broad Street.

Rev. T. Walton, dyspepsia and general debility; cured. 232 Hanover Street.

W. Forsyth's wife cured. India-rubber Works, Roxbury.

5

L. S. Hewett, dyspepsia, liver complaint, pain in the breast, and general debility; cured. 69 Princeton Street.

L. Perron's wife, cancer in the breast; cured. 132 Endicott Street.

C. V. Skinner, consumption; cured. Cambridgeport. Reference: M. M. Chick, 334 Washington Street.

Eliza Capen, erysipelas; cured. United States Hotel.

William A. Peters, debility; cured. Fourth Street.

Nathan A. Putnam, general wasting away of the whole body; cured. 28 Chestnut Street.

William C. Murphy's wife, disease peculiar to her sex; cured. Museum Exchange Saloon, Tremont Street.

F. N. Barlow, consumption; cured. Newport, Rhode Island. Boat Builder.

Miss M. Ennis, pimples on the face; cured. 9 French Street.

A. L. Hutchinson, scrofula; cured. South Reading, Mass.

C. Connell, shortness of breath, lungs almost gone; cured. Maverick Street, Chelsea.

D. Murphy, pimples on the face; cured. 83 Cove Street.

John W. Kane, general debility; cured. Sharon, Mass.

A. R. White, Esq., consumption and derangement of the nervous system; cured.

Mrs. M. A. H. Walker, ulcerated sore leg; cured. 15 Pearl Street, Portland, Maine.

T. C. Kenny, dyspepsia, pain in the breast, loss of appetite, nervousness, general debility, and constipation; cured. 33 Princeton Street.

William Fenby, dyspepsia, pain in the chest, back, shoulders, side, and head, with a melancholy and gloomy state of mind; cured. Engineer Boston Cordage Co.

A. Guerney, consumption; cured. Lynn, Mass.

E. D. Maglathlin, pimples on face; cured. Foreman for Badger & Bailey, Commercial Wharf.

Miss M. Bright, pimples on the face; cured. Watertown, Mass.

T. C. Pazolt, inflammation of the eyes; cured. 360 Washington Street.

Mrs. C. Donovan, blindness; cured. 82 Water Street, Charlestown, Mass.

Mr. T. Dolon, debility; cured. Guild & White's Tannery, Roxbury Mass.

C. E. Fitcham, pimples on face; cured. Boston & Maine R. R. Freight-office.

Alonzo Lewis, the Lynn Bard, cured of dyspepsia.

Miss Toplin, cough and paralysis; cured. 17 Merrimac Street.

Mr. J. H. Dyer, general debility and disease of blood; cured. Quincy Market.

Mr. H. Wilson, large tumor removed without the use of the knife; cured. —— Street, Cambridge.

Miss Lucy Powers, consumption; cured. Dover Street.

NEW YORK AND VICINITY.

W. Cameron, consumption; cured. Engineer Harlem Railroad Shop, Fourth Avenue.

Peter Miller, fistula; cured. Macdougal Street Bell-tower, New York.

W. Weaver, bronchitis; cured. 182 Lawrence Street.

Mrs. Moore, tape-worm; cured. 92 West Nineteenth Street.

Mrs. Judson, erysipelas; cured. Flatbush Avenue.

Mr. Rinkin's son, hip-joint disease; cured. 117 Fifth Street.

P. Brady, consumption, with ulcers on his body; cured. 254 East Eighteenth Street.

Mrs. E. Blanche's son, consumption; cured. 346 Greenwich Street.

Jaran Borke's wife, inward piles, of five years' standing; cured. Taylor's Saloon, Broadway.

G. Trunkett's son, fits; cured. Member of Stewart's Band.

John Johnson, consumption; cured. Master of the British Brig Blackburn.

P. B. Howard's wife, consumption; cured. 97 Henry Street, Brooklyn.

P. Fitzsimmons' daughter, spasms; cured. Corner of Pacific St. and Grand Avenue, Brooklyn.

Alfred Brown, six tumors; cured. 16 High Street, Brooklyn.

E. Fry, rheumatism and general debility; cured. Navy-yard, Brooklyn.

John Mott, cured of affection of the lungs, dyspepsia, costiveness, etc. 226 Fulton Street, Brooklyn.

Bernard McCannon, cured of cough, spitting, pain in the back. Pacific Street, near Grand Avenue, Brooklyn.

Miss Keeler, daughter of Michael Keeler, ex-Supervisor, of Brooklyn, cured of consumption, and general debility.

P. McDonald, cured of general debility, 161 John Street, Brooklyn.

Dennis Callagham, cured of night-sweats, bad cough, debility, emaciation, etc. Brooklyn.

William A. Brown, cured of general debility and disease of the blood. Navy-yard, Brooklyn.

J. M. Rawan, cured of consumption. 118 Duffield St., Brooklyn.

G. D. Abott, cured of dyspepsia and general debility. 29 Broadway, New York.

W. J. Beathe, 122 East Twenty-eighth Street, New York. Liver complaint.

Mrs. W. Allen, 704 Eighth Avenue. Consumption.

Mr. Parkin, 224 Cherry Street, New York. Rheumatism.

E. Otis, Ship Carpenter, Navy-yard. Scrofula.

W. H. Hiller, Williamsburg. Dyspepsia.

F. Weber, 239 Smith Street, Brooklyn. Spasmodic fits.

John Trimble, Machinist, at McLeads & Co.'s Establishment, South Brooklyn. Catarrh.

J. C. Calhound, cured of dyspepsia. 234 Pearl Street, Brooklyn.

George H. Jarvis, cured of disease of the blood. 155 Fulton St., Brooklyn.

Ben. Ryer, cured of scrofula. 8 Vine Street, Brooklyn.

Mrs. Holden, cured of ulcerated sore leg. 251 West Twelfth St.

P. J. Martin, cured of consumption. 274 Atlanta St., Brooklyn.

Mrs. Chase's son, cured of consumption. 587 Fulton St., Brooklyn.

S. Baldson, cured of scrofulous eruptions on the face. Union Hotel, Brooklyn.

George Cook, cured of rheumatism. 252 Gold Street, Brooklyn.

William Fortune, cured of scrofula. 70 Main Street, Brooklyn.

ST. LOUIS AND VICINITY.

Valentine Kapf, cured of scurvy.

B. A. Pagels, cured of rheumatism. 50 Olive Street.

William C. Jameson, cured of consumption. Pilot.

John Busch, cured of pimples on the face. Fourth St., St. Louis.

Jane Williams, cured of prolapsus uteri. Ninth Street.

J. B. Job, cured of disease of the blood. Alton, Illinois.

J. F. Simmon's wife, cured of disease peculiar to her sex. Corner of Seventh and Morgan Streets.

A. H. Conger, cured of general debility, pain in the back, breast, etc. Second Street.

G. W. McClure, late Capt. 195th Ill. Inf., cured of consumption.

W. P. Emery, Lindell Hotel, cured.

William McBride, Pilot, cured of dyspepsia.

B. N. Thompson, cured of sore throat and salivated sore mouth. Corner of Seventh Street and Washington Avenue.

• Jacob Gross's daughter, cured of St. Vitus' dance. Broadway.

W. B. Turner, cured of cancer. Center Township.

John Patrick, cured of dyspepsia and liver complaint. Employe of G. F. Filley, Main Street.

Miss K. Stemberg, cured of general debility, pain in the back, lassitude of the muscular system, disease of the heart, etc.

M. Gautair, cured of dyspepsia. 17 Lumber Street.

O. G. Rule, Foreman St. Louis Shot-tower, cured of dyspepsia and liver complaint. Residence, Tenth Street.

Mrs. E. J. Bodris, wife of Mr. Bodris, Engineer of the O'Fallon Mills, St. Louis, cured of rheumatism. 214 Clark Avenue.

James Crowley, East St. Louis, cured of consumption.

Thomas Clary, cured of consumption. Sworn to before me, this second day of February, 1865. JOHN M. YOUNG, J. P.

A. M. Henderson, Conductor on Ohio and Mississippi Railroad.

Mrs. Howard, cured of general debility. Thirteenth Street, between Webster and Chambers.

Miss P. Gustis, cured of blindness. Washington Street.

Mr. Hinkley, dyspepsia, cough, pain in the breast, general debility, etc., cured. 1037 Seventh Street.

James McGinnis, Pilot on the Mississippi, his son cured.

P. Manley, cured of erysipelas. 27 Main Street.

James Green, cured of consumption. Watchman on board the Joseph Gartside.

N. B. Turner's son, cured of cancer. 50 Center Street.

Charlotte Roberts, cured of scrofula. Venice, Illinois.

John Bush, cured of pimples on the face. Fourth Street.

Joseph Mulhall, cured of dyspepsia and debility. Corner of Morgan Street and Ewing Avenue.

S. Baffe's wife, cured of inward bleeding piles. Locust Street.

Mrs. C. Watson's daughter, cured of sore eyes. Washington Av.

A. B. Osborne's daughter, cured of general debility. St. Louis.

Mrs. Bingham's child, cured of scrofula. Twelfth St., St. Louis.

Delphy Ramsey, cured of rheumatism. Morgan Street.

George Jones, Everett House, cured of scrofula.

CINCINNATI AND VICINITY.

James Entwistle, cured of bronchitis. Corner of Sixth and Walnut Streets.

Mrs. Beech, Madison St., Covington, Kentucky, cured of catarrh, cough, and debility.

Mrs. Thomas, 478 West Ninth Street, cured.

E. M. Miller, Enquirer Building, cured of constipation and liver complaint.

T. Edwards, 437 Columbia Street, cured of shortness of breath, cough, pain in the breast, etc.

Henry Cutter, 612 Race Street, cured.

Mrs. Cochrain, Fourth Street, Covington, Kentucky, cured.

F. Masser, South Covington; his four children cured of a dreadful blood disease.

William Fenton, Justice of the Peace, Seventeenth Ward, cured.

C. Strubbe, 468 Main Street, cured. Sworn to before me, this thirteenth day of January, 1866.   JOHN W. CARTER, J. P.

Rev. H. Powell's wife, cured of chronic inflammation of the stomach, torpid liver, debility, etc. 37 New Street.

Mrs. Wilkeson, member of the Carr Street Church, cured of a chronic complaint.

Miss A. Evans, 114 Barr Street, cured of general debility, cough, etc.

Mr. J. Schwab, 211 Walnut Street, cured.

' L. Creighton, Columbia, cured of debility.

Levi Baxter, Morrow, O., cured.

F. M. Henley, Foreman O. & M. Machine Shop, cured of humorous eruptions, pimples, blotches, and boils.

Mr. A. Hamilton's lady, cured. Ticket Agent, L. M. R. R.

From Phil. Tieman's Brother-in-law:

INDIAN HERB DOCTOR—*Dear Sir:* I take pleasure in informing you that your medicine has been the means of saving my life. I and a fistula so bad that no medicine which I could procure did me any good, until my attention was drawn to the virtues of your medicine, by the use of which I have been restored. I have gained twenty-one pounds of flesh in three weeks.

JOHN H. FILLENEY, 264 *Vine Street.*

W. J. Rusk, owner and Captain of Steamer St. Cloud, cured of general debility, dyspepsia, palpitation of the heart, weak lungs, etc.

R. Ware, 550 Elm Street, cured.

J. Bane, 187 Cutter Street, cured of catarrh.

Mrs. A. E. Frost, Covington, Kentucky, cured of catarrh and offensive breath.

Mrs. Otto, of Lawrenceburg, Indiana, cured of bleeding piles.

Peter Kort, cured of liver complaint with blotches on the skin. Sworn to and subscribed before me, this twelfth day of February, 1866.   BENJAMIN C. TRUE, J. P.

T. Underwood, of Glendale, cured of debility.

Miss N. Hoff, corner of Eighth and Elm, cured.

Mr. Kelly, 25 Court Street, cured of asthma.

Mr. T. Twichell, 118 Richmond Street, cured of anguia pectoris, or neuralgic affection of the heart.

G. W. Catrell, cured of gravel.   69 Walnut Street.

With the above evidences of my claim to the gratitude of a portion of my fellow-beings, and a becoming consciousness that my mission in life, thus far, has not been unproductive of good, I will close.

It was not my intention to relate the incidents of my life, but only that portion which bore upon the oppression and indignity of which I was the victim. I trust that there is yet before me a long professional career, for I am young, hopeful, and anxious to ameliorate, as far as my humble ability will aid me, the sufferings of humanity.

But for the wanton defamation of my reputation, and the indignity and outrage to my person, I should never have appeared in this guise before the public; a due regard, however, to a name and fame that, from my earliest remembrance, I have endeavored to preserve unsullied, has induced the above narrative and statement of facts. How far I have succeeded in establishing an unblemished reputation, and exposing malignant jealousy, tyranny, and oppression, I leave with those who have perused the foregoing pages to determine; and in the belief that their verdict will not be an unfavorable one, I subscribe myself their devoted servant,

FRANCIS TUMBLETY.

I have said that the good physician~is known by his works, and I can flatter myself that but few practitioners can exhibit so fair a record as myself. I have already furnished the reader with what would be ordinarily deemed sufficient evidence of the success of my practice, but in looking over my portfolio, I find the subjoined; and as the writers enjoy distinguished positions in their respective localities, and can vouch for their authenticity, I have deemed fit to append these voluntary contributions.

The first is from a highly-respectable citizen of London, C. W., addressed to the editor of the *Free Press.* It is necessary for me to state that the first intimation I received of Mr. Ferguson's case being made public, was by his own act, as it met my eye in print:

To the Editor of the Free Press :

My Dear Sir—Permit me through the very valuable columns of your paper to say that on last Good Friday I called at Mr. Strong's Hotel in this city, and saw a person there who applied to Dr. Tumblety for relief from a disease of scrofula; the person was covered nearly from head to foot. He was then in the employment of R. Tomilson, chandler, of this city. The Doctor asked him $5 for a cure; the person went to his employer for the money, and returned soon afterward, stating, if the Doctor would effect the cure, he would give him $10; the Doctor agreed to his proposal. I saw the person sixteen days afterward, he was almost entirely well, and told me he was able to work. The change effected on the person was such as no one could describe.

I also saw another person who had not less than twelve running ulcers upon his leg—a farmer from the country—the state of his leg was fearful. Dr. Tumblety also cured him within three weeks. The person told me he had spent hundreds of dollars with other physicians, who invariably failed to afford him relief. I take the liberty of mentioning these things for the benefit of the public. I must confess, at the same time, that I have had my prejudices against people from the "other side"—frequently coming here, and under various pretexts, deceiving our people; yet I am constrained to give the highest credit to Dr. Tumblety for his pretensions from the people that have been brought under my notice. I recommend all who are troubled with diseases to consult him.

My dear sir, I remain yours truly, JAMES FERGUSON.
LONDON, *April* 12, 1853.

The next was also a hearty and gratuitous contribution from a justly-celebrated Canadian divine. It speaks for itself:

IONA, *May* 31, 1856.

DR. F. TUMBLETY, *Hamilton, C. W.;*

Dear Sir—Rev. James Silcox, of the Township of Southwold, County of Elgin, C. W., has requested me to state to you, that from the use of your Vegetable Medicines, he has cured himself of a very bad cough of several years' standing. Also, from the use of the same he cured his little boy, who was thought to have consumption.

Rev. J. Silcox wished me to state to you that he is perfectly willing you shall make use of this as you may think proper.

I remain your obedient servant, GEORGE SHARP,
Methodist Minister.

My third comes down to a later date, and embodies the testimonial of one of the most popular captains known in Buffalo. It was inserted by him in the *Courier* of that city:

I have been taking more or less medicines from the physicians of Buffalo for over three years, for consumption, asthma, cough, debility, and want of nervous energy, and could get no good, but continued to decline; till at last I could scarcely walk alone, and had to give up business entirely, never expecting to resume it; but thanks to Dr. Tumblety, I am now in a way to recover. I have been using his medicines three weeks, and am improving in every respect.

A. PRATT,
BUFFALO, *February* 14, 1859. *Captain Steamer Globe.*

I owe a word of apology to the reader for introducing the above, but as I am certain that this pamphlet will be circulated freely in the communities wherein the above three gentlemen reside, I feel that I shall possess the testimony and hearty indorsement of three unimpeachable witnesses on behalf of my professional ability and successful practice.

I might, were I so minded, adduce another accumulation of corroborative testimony from reliable parties in this city, Cincinnati—ladies and gentlemen of the most unimpeachable veracity, who, unsolicited and in a pure spirit of philanthropy, in the desire to comfort and aid those who are similarly afflicted, have made known their cases, and the benefit derived from my treatment, when, in most instances, almost hope had been abandoned—but I think that the reader will agree with me that further evidence is unnecessary, so I will not again recur to the subject.

A few more remarks will not be inapplicable concerning my arrest, and the presumed cause, for it was all presumption, and the arrangement was so mystified and befogged, that at the time I was almost tempted to question my own identity. Indeed, I was somewhat in the same predicament of the rustic wagoner, who while asleep, some rogues unhitched the team and carried them off.

Awakening soon after he rubbed his eyes in a state of bewilderment, and after a few minutes intense cogitation, was delivered of the following soliloquy:

"Am I Hodge, or aint I Hodge? If I am Hodge, I've lost four spanking fine horses. If I aint Hodge, I've found a wagon."

In my case, however, if I lost my identity, I discovered something far less agreeable than a wagon, in the shape of the Old Capitol Prison.

The application to the above is, that I was first suspected of being the friend, associate, and partner of the notorious Herrold, and consequently that I must have been privy to the project of the assassination. Then the article quoted from a St. Louis paper, announced me as Dr. Blackburn, and this idea derived additional force by being flashed broadcast upon the telegraph wires. The fact is, my arrest was one of those open-handed acts of wantonness that could only spring from a reckless and irresponsible official, wielding absolute authority, and without the pale of the fear of God or of mankind.

Now that the wounds of this so lately distracted country are rapidly healing under the benignant influence of peace, and happily the constitutional right and liberty of the citizen is again restored, should it not be a serious question that must come home to every individual, to guard for the future against such tyranny and oppression as were practiced with so much impunity by the Secretary of War. My case might, under a similar state of affairs, be yours; no man, however innocent, can be sure of escaping the foul wrong which, with me, resulted in great pecuniary loss, bodily and mental suffering, and a broken constitution. I am aware that in a time of civil war, and a war, too, in which it required the full force and power of the Government to put down one of the most formidable rebellions that ever arrayed itself against the constituted authorities, that extreme measures are necessary, but surely the lives of innocent people are not to be jeopardized with such capricious indifference.

The chronicles of Ireland will furnish many instances of undue harshness exercised during troubled times, and the suspension of the writ of *habeas corpus*, but I challenge the record to produce such a flagrant abuse of power, and wanton outrage of the liberty of the citizen, as was exemplified in my case, and I may say hundreds, if not thousands of others. Under these circumstances, is it not a dangerous precedent to allow the prime minister of these un-American atrocities to escape a just and wholesome castigation for his treasonable practices against the Constitution, in the persons of those who should be protected in its broad fold. I do not write in a vindictive spirit; Heaven knows that were I alone the sufferer, I would endure, and rest content with the vindication of my name and fame from the odious calumnies which were so heedlessly and upon no foundation cast upon me; but the names of my co-mates are legion, and I feel that the public good demands an *example* for all future tyrants, who, dressed in the brief garb of authority, may take advantage of precedent to play the same fantastic tricks at the expense of right, justice, humanity, and liberty.

And, yet, the man's love of office is wonderful; for he holds on with a tenacity—and certainly with greater damage to the subject—as the barnacle to the bottom of the ship. No public man was more hated than Edwin Stanton; at the present time, no one is so despised. He will leave a name in history, but beside it that of any other who figured in the late eventful epoch, will be respectable.

It is not easy to make a catalogue of great men, but it is easy to see how, from time to time, the standard of greatness changes. A military general can hardly ever again enjoy the exclusive kind of fame that once belonged to him. " The victories of peace are beginning to supply heroes for the laurel as well as those of war." Still the wise and benignant statesman, and the victorious general, will live in the grateful remembrance of their countrymen, while the cruel despot of the day will go down to posterity cursed with the immortality that encircles the name of Nero.

It is now within a few days of the anniversary of my arrest. Looking back over the year that has passed, the light and shadow of good and ill flits before me in sunny and somber hues, and bygones are softened by the soothing hand of time. A year ago, and I stood unconsciously upon the threshold of a bastile. It was the opening of May, that sweet season so beautifully described in Solomon's song: " The time of the singing of birds is come, and the voice of the turtle is heard in the land."

In this buoyant and festive season, when the earth is carpeted with its tenderest green, and the poetry of nature is realized in the many-tinted buds that already perfume the soft Southern breeze; when the birds are singing, the cattle lowing, the trees blossoming, the brooks gurgling, the rivers flowing, the sun shining, and the clouds flying, in this month of beautiful May, when the whole world is quickened and kindled, and life, like nature, assumes its holiday attire, it was hard indeed to be consigned by a ruthless and arbitrary power to the gloom of a state dungeon, and the dark speculation of an uncertain future. But the night is past, the reign of terror that cast its shadow across the blue ether, and reflected an ominous cloud upon the fair land, is no more.. We have fallen upon happier

times, upon peaceful and tranquil days. Let us hope
that the dark page of history will, like " the uses of
adversity," prove a jewel in the shape of a warning
to guide the future course of the nation; and that
even now as the sun of liberty is blended with the
sunshine of May, so may its bright and joyous light
never again be dimmed, but remain with us in all its
pristine beauty.

After I had laid down my pen, I unfolded a morning paper that, as usual, was placed upon my table,
and there read the startling intelligence that the
cholera had been brought to the shores of America by
an overcrowded passenger ship. The news was sufficiently exciting to induce me to address the reader
a few concluding remarks upon what bids fair to be
the engrossing and all-absorbing topic of the day.
Perhaps one of the greatest, as it certainly has been
the most benevolent act of the present ruler of France,
was the tracing this dreadful scourge to its source, in
the vast congregation of pilgrims who flock to the
shrine of Mahomet, who, being necessarily compelled
to crowd together in unwholesome masses, exposed to
a fetid atmosphere, with impure diet, and the impossibility of indulging in the necessary ablutions so in-
dispensable to a healthy condition, engender disease,
which, in that climate especially, assumes a malignant
form, and is thus spread until its baleful influence is
felt, although, of course, in a modified form, throughout
the civilized world.

Now, far beyond the precincts of Mecca a like cause
must necessarily produce a similar effect; nor can I
conceive a situation more rife for breeding the disease
than an overcrowded emigrant ship, where a mass of

over a thousand ill-assorted persons are crowded together within the contracted, badly-ventilated, and pestiferous atmosphere of a steerage. Indeed, it has frequently been a matter of surprise to me that every breeze from the East, as it sweeps over these floating repositories of animal filth and misery, is not laden with infection.

These remarks are suggested in the hope that they may have the effect of allaying the fears and excitement of those who read them; for I can assure the reader that there is a mysterious influence which the mind exercises over the body, and experience proves that the fearful and most excitable portion of the community are invariably the first victims of contagious disorders. An even and temperate course of life, cleanliness, and moderate attention to the regular operations of nature, and a cheerful mind, are the best preventives for cholera; but should it come, nature has spread forth her boundless store of roots and herbs to combat the Asiatic scourge, for here her resources are boundless; and to him who has studied her, there is life, health, and vigor in her simple teaching. Has it never struck the reader that the untutored Indian, with all his bad habits, has suffered so little in the periodical visits of this particular scourge? The reason is as simple as it is significant. The Indian experiences one blessing in being exempt from the baleful influence of old medical fogies. For his ailments he relies upon the antidotes which nature has spread before him, and which first instinct, and then tradition, has taught him the use of; hence it is, that while contagion and death has desolated alike the hovel and the palace of civilization, the child of the forest in his

wigwam walks erect, fearless of an enemy which, if it
attack him, he knows he can combat with success.

As I write, the name of the celebrated phrenologist,
Professor Fowler, catches my eye.   He is, I perceive,
advertised to deliver a series of lectures in this city
of Cincinnati; and this recalls a not unpleasant reminiscence, in which the Professor is identified.   I became acquainted with him some years since, while we
were each pursuing our professional avocation, and I
have reason to hope that the friendly sentiment with
which he imbued me was, in a measure, reciprocated.
I admire a man of science; for genius is a god-like
gift, more precious than ancestral honors or the much-
coveted wealth of gold and silver.   Professor Fowler
is the first, as he is the most celebrated, in his profession; and I here take pleasure in adding my tribute
to the many of which he is justly the recipient.   His
is a bold, and in many respects, an original theory,
and the truth has been pretty fairly illustrated by
continued success.

And here I am, as it were, once again inadvertently
led to the contemplation of the old and, in many respects, ridiculous practice insisted upon by the ancient
faculty, who really appear to imagine that prejudice
is a holy principle, if sanctified by age.   In no point
do they hold with more tenacious determination, than
in blood-letting, which by many is esteemed a remedy
for all the ills that afflict humanity.   Dr. Smollet, in
his admirable translation of Le Sage's "Gil Blas,"
shows up, in inimitable satirical style, the absurdity of
this destructive course.   Dr. Sangrado was but a type
of the great mass of our modern M. D.'s, who continue

to extract the life-blood of their patients in spite of nature and common sense.

In an excellent treatise upon this subject, the eminent Dr. Coggswell said that the disuse of the lancet and blisters is demanded both by humanity and science. Is it not a mistake to suppose that a kettle of boiling water (the inflamed blood) will cease to boil by dipping out a part of it? Is it not a mistake to suppose that blisters and rubefacients will remove inflammation, when they virtually superadd one inflammation to another? But I fear that philosophy, or the most lucid reasoning, will fail with the indomitable prejudice of the majority of the old-time practitioners, who, following the example of Dr. Sangrado, will still go on blood-letting and sowing a profitable harvest for the undertaker and the sexton.

In the testimonials I have adduced, there are but very few cases which were not treated by the regular practitioners before my services were called into requisition, and, therefore, to the most obtuse it must be apparent, the superiority of my treatment. In the category there are cases which were so desperate that the last lingering hope of life was abandoned, and I am happy to know that there are many at this time who regard me with grateful remembrance, as having snatched them from the grave. I never knowingly deceive a patient; my motto is, and always has been, to deal frankly and honestly with all who consult me. The following notice, which appears in the Woodstock C. W. *Spirit of the Times*, is equally applicable at the present time:

" Invalids, and all those suffering under lingering

diseases, will find it to their interest to give the Indian Doctor a call. If he can do you no good, he will frankly tell you so, and not charge you for advice."

While there is life there is hope, but there are cases in which the physician will best exercise the attribute of mercy by preparing the unfortunate sufferer for that final dissolution, which the experienced practitioner but too well can perceive, must come surely and speedily.

www.ingramcontent.com/pod-product-compliance
Lightning Source LLC
Chambersburg PA
CBHW032355020726
47499CB00008B/2751